HUNG OVER

HUNG OVER

A TIM SIMPSON MYSTERY

John Malcolm

St. Martin's Press
New York

Extract from *Justine* by Lawrence Durrell
is reproduced by kind permission of Faber & Faber Ltd

The quotation from 'Lines on a Young Lady's
Photograph Album' by Philip Larkin is reprinted
from *The Less Deceived* by permission of the
Marvell Press, England and Australia

Library of Congress Cataloging-in-Publication Data

Malcolm, John
Hung over / John Malcolm.
p.   cm.
"A Thomas Dunne book."
ISBN 0-312-13514-9 (hardcover)
1. Simpson, Tim (Fictitious character)—Fiction.   2. Art—
Collectors and collecting—Fiction.   I. Title.
PR6063.A362H86   1995
823'.914—dc20   95-22842   CIP

First published in Great Britain by HarperCollins*Publishers*

First U.S. Edition: September 1995
10 9 8 7 6 5 4 3 2 1

HUNG OVER

CHAPTER 1

'We will have to move quickly,' Jeremy White barked at me, raising a sharp finger-spike to emphasize his point. 'Without delay. This opportunity must be grasped tenaciously. At once.'

His voice was painfully penetrating as he struck a dramatic stance; I flinched, silently wishing that he didn't always have to be so bloody theatrical about everything.

'I suppose it must.' My words seemed to come from another person nearby, a person whose diction was strained and hoarse.

He flicked a straying switch of blond hair back into place with a flash of snowy shirt cuff secured by a prominent oval of gold linking. His eyes widened as he swivelled his intent, challenging stare upon me. 'One has got to get cracking pretty smartly these days if the race is to be won. There's some mighty strong runners amongst the opposition.'

'I'm sure you're right,' I responded mournfully, trying not to wince visibly or move my head from the vertical. Jeremy is impossibly strident once he's got a bee under his bonnet.

'We're under starter's orders. The flag is up.' There was an increase in volume, as though I wasn't hearing properly. 'It's time for the off. The odds will lengthen for every day that's lost.'

'Oh, do put a sock in it, please, Jeremy.'

This entreaty knitted his bleached brows into an injured scowl. I ignored it. I wasn't feeling well. My throat was dry, my head throbbed and there was a lump on my shin that felt about the size of an ostrich egg. My eyes were both painful and bloodshot. Concentrated thought was impossible. Yet here was Jeremy, braying away about buying the Crockingham Collection and peppering his speech with horse racing metaphors. I didn't want to buy the Crockingham Collection. I didn't want White's Art Fund to buy it, either. I'm not at all horsy. I was intrigued by the card I'd left lying on my desk.

5

I wished to heaven that he would calm down.

'It seems to me,' he said fretfully, leaning back against the mock-mantelpiece over his blocked office fireplace and shoving both hands into his striped jacket pockets like a politician on a rostrum, 'that, if I may say so, you are showing a singular lack of enthusiasm. A singular lack of enthusiasm. I had been hoping for a positive, even an enthusiastic, response.' He cocked his head forward to look at me disapprovingly. 'I imagined you would be chafing at the bit when I told you about this one. Yoicks and tally ho; I sprang to the saddle and Jorrocks and he – that sort of thing. Wordsworth, isn't it?'

'Browning,' I ground out in hoarse and testy correction. 'The stirrup, not the saddle. Joris, not Jorrocks. "I sprang to the stirrup, and Joris, and he."'

I nearly went on to say that bringing good news, whether from Aix to Ghent, or vice versa, and by horse at that, was not appropriate to the information he had just imparted, but he was already in full interruptory flight.

'Your manner is, however, not to put too fine a point on it, dank. Negatively dank. By definition, therefore, dark, damp and discouraging. I'm very disappointed.'

'I've got a hangover.'

'Ha!' His eyes whitened and his nose went up, like a hunter's to the distant horn. 'A hangover! A hangover! I knew it! Damn it, I knew, from the moment you walked in this morning, that you were well below par! Well below par! And that alcohol poisoning would almost certainly be the explanation.'

I closed my eyes wearily, bringing blessed relief for a moment, then opened them again, which made me feel dizzy. This was alarming; it was quite clear that an inadvertent sideways movement of my head might cause it to snap off at the root. 'What you mean is that you knew damned well that I was at the Old Rugby Club dinner at the Savoy Grill last night.'

He bridled with a visible jerk, causing his Eton tie to spring from its moorings under his pinstriped jacket and swing in abandon across his chest. 'Not necessarily. Not necessarily at all! I didn't know that. It did not take prior knowledge to deduce your condition today!' He drew himself up, his shoulder nearly dislodging the oil painting of a three-master with stretched sails on the wall behind him, above his bogus fireplace. His voice rose to its most hectoring, pompous tone. 'I really think it is

6

time you paused to consider, you know. Really I do, Tim. You left college many years ago. There comes a time when one has to desist from these juvenile thrashes and behave responsibly. Responsibly. Really one does. Coming to work looking like something the cat dragged in after a night of delinquent alcoholic indulgence is simply not on for a senior member of the bank.' He gestured at the other man in the room to prevent me from retorting that he was lucky to see me at all. 'What do you think, Geoffrey?'

Geoffrey Price, our chief accountant, grinned at me. 'Good night, was it, Tim?'

I managed a smile back at him. 'Bloody marvellous. Head like a badger this morning.'

'That's my boy.'

'Really!' Jeremy always feigns personal injury when challenged on a pet project or baulked of smooth passage in some way. You'd think he'd never overdone it at the Yacht Club himself. 'I'm even more disappointed, really I am. It is quite wrong to condone his behaviour, Geoffrey! We have important work to do.' He glowered back at me. 'You've not been listening to me properly at all, have you? I've been wasting my time. I suppose you didn't get home until some godforsaken hour of the morning, did you?'

'I don't remember.'

'Good grief! As bad as that! What on earth did Sue say?'

'Haven't the faintest idea, Jeremy. I must have passed out on the sofa. She'd gone to work when I surfaced this morning.'

'Disgraceful! Appalling! My goodness, you'll get an earful when you get home. If she's still there.'

'Oh, I don't know, Jeremy. She must have dressed the wound on my shin because it was bandaged when I woke this morning and I certainly don't remember putting one on.'

'Wound on your shin?' His eyes bulged as he stared down at my trouserleg. 'What wound on your shin? For God's sake, you didn't start playing dining room rugby at some point during the proceedings, did you? Not in the Savoy Grill?'

I shook my head, causing another stab of agony, and quickly held it still. 'Oh, no, nothing like that. The dinner went relatively quietly. Lot of older jossers present. Ancient Blues, you know. Well, relatively quietly; the old codgers were pretty lively themselves. No, the shin must have happened while we of the younger element were trying to drop goals over Waterloo Bridge.'

He gave a gasp of horror. 'Drop goals? Over Waterloo Bridge? At night? Impossible! How on earth?'

'From the roadway below, Jeremy. Quite difficult, actually, but it seemed like a good idea at the time. Someone always brings a few rugby balls to that kind of hooley. I must have collided with a bollard or something doing a run-up, but Dickie Bulverhythe – he was a full-back, you know – got one clean over. Bloody marvellous kick, considering the circumstances. There's nothing like a bet with the Sattersthwaite boys to get Dickie going. Although there was heated argument about whether it bounced on the roadway or not. I think it was the fracas over his ball – it hit a passing lorry eventually – that must have brought the police along.'

'*The police?*' He clutched his head. 'Dear God, are we to be spared nothing from this brutal night of puerile bacchanalia? Don't tell me you'll be appearing at Bow Street on a charge? My God! What will the board say about that?'

His expression, under the thatch of blond hair now becoming much more disarrayed, was screwed into a contortion of alarm. I hastened to calm him.

'No, no, Jeremy. Nothing like that. Sporting crowd, the Metropolitan Police. They play rugby too, you know. They thought it was a hell of a joke. Especially as we had Nobby Roberts with us.'

His eyes bulged again; further out this time. 'Nobby? You mean Chief Inspector Roberts? From the Yard?'

'Yes. He nearly got one over the bridge, too. Damn good effort, it was. He was my guest, actually; Nobby didn't get his blue, as you know. He rather let his hair down last night. Unusual for Nobby, I must say. He's normally so sanctimonious about that sort of thing. He was in great form. Apparently, he'd got a big conviction at the Old Bailey yesterday afternoon – a villain called Banks, master of the underworld or something – the papers will be full of it today – and was in a celebratory mood. The rozzers cheered like mad when they recognized him and gave him great claps on the back. Last thing I saw of him, he was being led off to their van so they could all go to an appalling pub in Limehouse that stays open all night.'

'This is absolutely horrendous! Horrendous! Utter licentiousness! Even the police are out of control! The whole fabric of society is breaking down!'

Jeremy was going quite mottled. Geoffrey Price, however, who played cricket for his college and can keep up with almost any festivities known to sporting life, was chuckling openly. 'How smashing! Over Waterloo Bridge, eh? You mad dog, Tim. But didn't the force invite you lot along to Limehouse as well?'

'Oh, no. It was a private celebration. We were lucky to have Nobby with us at all. They nailed this Banks after practically the entire force worked like mad to get him. Violent and nasty, apparently. They probably had the chief constable standing rounds last night. Dickie and I went back to join some old chums in the Strand – the Sattersthwaites amongst others – and ended up at a club in Soho somewhere. There was a show of sorts, but I don't remember much about it; the champagne was terrible. Some kind soul must have loaded us into taxis home eventually.' I gave our superior a reproving look. 'If you had any Christian charity at all, Jeremy, you'd be laying on a gallon of strong black coffee.'

He grimaced. 'I suppose we shall get nothing useful out of you until we do.' He rang for his secretary. 'While we are arranging to anaesthetize your condition, however, could you explain just why you are being so bloody negative over the Crockingham Collection?'

I sighed. Actually, I couldn't; that morning my mind wasn't up to explanations. And the card on my desk was much more interesting; its cleverly-concealed message was teasing my brain.

'I just don't like it, Jeremy. A block purchase, I mean. All those horses all together, just like that. Art as a sort of bulk commodity; it offends me.'

'Don't like it? Don't like it? It's a golden opportunity! An assemblage of first-rate equestrian paintings and sculpture of the late nineteenth but mostly early twentieth centuries. The kind of thing the Art Fund has specialized in all along!' He quickly talked over the protest my opening mouth was about to utter. 'And we can have first crack at it. I thought you'd jump at the chance.'

His voice had gone petulant. Jeremy rather prides himself on being able to throw opportunities my way; opportunities which he is reluctant to follow up himself. The Art Fund we managed was a scheme to allow White's clients to invest in art without buying a Rembrandt themselves or running the mockery of their friends at their taste or perspicacity. It had done rather well, but had involved me in several somewhat unpleasant situations which Jeremy had done his best to avoid. In this case, the yachting pastime on the Solent which occupied Jeremy's free hours had led to a close contact with Philip Carberry, a member of the family who not only owned the Crockingham Collection but whose remaining, quite important investments, were handled by White's Bank. He could, he hinted, give Jeremy and the Art Fund first swing at buying the Collection, which, due to heavy losses at Lloyds, the family was probably going to have to sell. Hence our meeting that morning.

The coffee came, giving me an opportunity to think about how to answer him. We had never bought equestrian pieces before, but I knew that in his present mood he'd quickly discount that objection as an example of stuffy, hidebound lack of initiative. By the time I had filled a cup, put a lot of sugar in it, drunk it and refilled, I had come to the melancholy conclusion that there was little I could do to avoid Jeremy's demand that I at least toddle along and take a gander at the equine art works. After all, it *is* what I am supposed to do for the Fund; the only defence I could prepare was a possible shortage of cash with which to buy. Jeremy, however, had summoned Geoffrey Price along to cover that subject; I cocked an eye at him and, as if I didn't know, I said, 'How are we off for cash, Geoffrey?'

'We have it in abundance! Far too much of it!' Jeremy was well in advance of me.

Geoffrey nodded soberly. 'Rather cash-rich at present, Tim. And it looks as though, from a cash-is-king situation, we are headed for –'

'Cash is trash!' Jeremy was still bullish. And full of the latest jargon. 'We must use our money. Use it. There's no profit in leaving it on deposit. Not these days.'

I sighed again.

'Very well, Jeremy. I will go and inspect the goods. Then I will report back.'

'At last! At last!' He waved his cup in triumph. 'Well, don't look so hangdog, Tim! Try to seem willing! We have a chance to kill two birds with one stone! To help a good client out of a jam and make a scoop for the Art Fund! Good heavens above, what do I have to do to keep everyone on their toes in this place? We are here to invest. To invest! Not to sit about looking morbid, hanging on to our cash. Risk, risk, that is what merchant banking is all about. Eh? Eh?'

Geoffrey looked at me. I looked at Geoffrey. Neither of us said anything. My throat was still as dry as dust and the coffee was making my head hot. What I really needed was a long cold beer. I'm no soak and a reunion dinner once in a while doesn't make a man an alcoholic, but that morning I was definitely under the weather. If I'd been on proper form, I might have done better at dissuading Jeremy, but it's no good moralizing now, or blaming the Old Blues; it just happened that way.

'Well come along,' Jeremy bullied, 'I'm sure we've all got work to do. Off you go, Tim. Get along to the Crockingham Collection as soon as you can, while we've still got first option. Philip Carberry wants the whole thing to be kept strictly confidential at this stage. Strictly confidential. If word gets round that the Carberrys are selling up the Collection, he fears they'll suffer a credit landslide and all sorts of complications. So mum's the word. Understood?'

'Absolutely stumm, Jeremy.'

'Good. At least we're ahead of Christerby's this time.' Jeremy sounded pleased; you'd think we were in competition with the auction house in which we have a thirty per cent stake.

He handed me a card with Philip Carberry's name and details on it. The address was up in Suffolk. I nodded very carefully, put down my empty cup, and obediently left his office.

That, for me, was how the whole thing started.

Hung over.

CHAPTER 2

I got back to my own office, sat down at the desk, put my head in my hands, then rang Penny whose services, in the purely secretarial sense, I share with another worthy, for more coffee. She brought it within seconds.

'My goodness!' she said. 'You look like Daddy the morning after a hunt ball.'

I gave her, from a face still cupped in hands, what I hoped was a withering stare. Penny is a new girl at the bank, culled from an apparently inexhaustible pool of County girls White's Bank seems able to tap at will. Her father, who had given the place the once-over before approving us as employers, was a leathery old Johnny with a face tanned and seamed from a lifetime of riding horses through blizzards, broking stocks and drinking hard liquor. He looked about eighty years older than me, though he couldn't possibly have been. It wasn't a flattering comparison.

'I've put a lot of sugar in,' she said, helpfully.

Girls like Penny, fair-skinned, fair-haired, willowy but with wide hips, wide eyes and brisk schoolish manners, used to come to merchant banking to find healthy young men of good prospects with a view to marriage. Nowadays, they tend to witter on about their careers and whether the work you set them will help in their personal business development. They also pester for project material for a business diploma course geared towards becoming President of the Mitsubishi Corporation or, failing that, Governor of the Bank of England. It is very depressing. Fortunately, Penny is not one of these, nor does she seem to have any desire for additional responsibilities; she shares a flat near High Street Kensington with four other girls and is addicted to exhausting social amusements with eager, well-spoken escorts who she handles with cool expertise. It irks me to think how, before I was married and when I chased girls like Penny,

I had no idea how I was being manipulated; I thought then that I was in control of things. I see now that I was merely an irrelevant diversion for girls like Penny.

Age brings saddening self-knowledge.

'When will you be going up to Suffolk?' she demanded, brightly.

'Eh?'

'For the Crockingham Collection. You're going to buy it, aren't you?'

I closed my overheated eyes. I might have guessed that the bank's grapevine, like that of the proverbial factory floor, would be right up to date and that Penny would have her own branch line into it. Secretaries, provided they haven't fallen out with each other over some extraordinary and incomprehensible slight or rivalry, soon have their networks polished.

'No,' I said, opening my eyes again carefully and reaching for the coffee, 'I am not going to buy the Crockingham Collection. Nor are we, the bank, necessarily going to buy it. I am going to look at it and to judge whether it, or parts of it, are suitable.'

'But Claire says that Jeremy is frightfully keen,' she said, as though that settled everything.

Claire is Jeremy's current secretary. My stare, I hoped, within its pain-fringed limitations, became a glare. 'That has no bearing,' I said, 'on anything at all. No bearing whatsoever.'

'No, Tim, of course not.'

The tone had quickly turned suspiciously sweet. I took a draught of the coffee, which was excellent, and modified my glare a little. Suddenly, I was conscious of the resemblance to her father. 'The Art Fund,' I said, 'makes its decisions after recommendation by one of the trustees. Not always, but usually, me.'

'Of course, Tim.'

'And may I remind you that, like all transactions and even potential transactions at this bank, the affairs and recommendations of the Art Fund are a matter for absolute secrecy and discretion.'

'Oh, absolutely.'

My eyes narrowed, but her face was expressionless. Actually, girls like Penny are brought up on a steady diet of absolute secrecy and discretion, especially where the business of broker fathers is involved. Within limits, of course. While they wouldn't blab to the outside world about things which they knew could lead to trouble, it's not as if they aren't part of an inner circle which might, under certain circumstances, discuss something with a view to mutual personal advantage.

Now I'm being cynical.

'It could be very embarrassing,' I burbled on, 'if the outside world got to know of a client's or of the bank's interest or intentions in a way which might affect the value of the object of those intentions. Or of similar commodities on the free market.'

'That's what they said on our induction course.'

I groaned. All joining staff get a sort of basic training-cum-obstacle course from the bank's personnel department. I was the embodiment of the Heavy Bore in repeating the obvious. What was more, the other worthy for whom Penny acted as secretary was involved in dealing and insurance in ways which made discretion an imperative.

'I'm sorry,' I said. 'I'm not at my brightest this morning.'

She smiled. 'Would you like some more aspirin?'

'No, thanks. I've taken enough aspirin to dilute my blood down to dishwater.'

'Don't you think much of the Crockingham Collection?'

'I don't know yet,' I said. 'I've never seen it. But I think it rather depends on whether you're keen on a one-eyed horse painter from Norwich or not.'

She gazed at me in puzzlement. I gave her an enigmatic stare and left her to work it out for herself; they say that youth needs challenges. My attention was already wandering back to the open envelope and card on my desk.

'Thanks for the coffee,' I said.

She gave up mentally wrestling with the one-eyed horse painter allusion and gestured vaguely. 'Nice card,' she said. Her smile was a bit fixed.

'Indeed.'

'I didn't know that you were keen on motor racing.'

'I'm not.'

'A boyfriend of mine once had a Bugatti. He took me to a vintage car rally in it.'

'Lucky fellow.'

'It was frightfully uncomfortable. And the people were boring. Really, really, seriously boring. They talked about con rods and sprockets and things like that all day.'

14

'Poor chap; I expect he hoped you'd be stimulated by speed. In its mature and expensive form, of course.'

Her eyebrows furrowed slightly. She gave me another long look, pursed her rather full, attractive lips, then walked carefully towards the door. Her father had trained her well. If the stirrup cups I'd been offered on the rare occasions I'd attended hunts or riding events were anything to go by, he must have a cast iron liver by now.

'Hang on,' I called after her. 'Don't toddle off just yet.'

She paused and turned back towards me with just a tinge of disapproval in her expression.

'Go through the *Art Sales Index*,' I ordered, 'and give me the salient figures on sales of paintings by Munnings over the last ten years.'

She glanced in surprise at the bound volumes and publications which line the shelves of my office; volumes of sales records and auction catalogues, reference books and the Royal Academy's illustrated Summer Exhibition catalogues going back to the year Josh Reynolds squeezed his first tube.

'Munnings?'

'Yes, Munnings. Sir Alfred of that ilk.' I smiled at her. 'The one-eyed horse painter from Norwich.'

Her equestrian father, I thought, would almost certainly have introduced her to Munnings. But not as a one-eyed horse painter from Norwich. She raised her eyebrows, nodded understandingly, then frowned a little once more in query.

'Did he really have only one eye?'

'He did. And, even so, still became President of the Royal Academy. Which has sparked strong opinions from both friends and enemies of that august institution.'

'All right.' Her disapproval had been replaced by just a hint of enthusiasm. 'I have to finish some work I was given first thing, then I'll come back and do that.'

'Good girl.'

She put her head on one side, considered, then went out springily. Art market research makes a welcome change from debentures.

At last I had the office to myself.

The card was about six inches by eight, with a blue-framed surround. It depicted a painting of a dated motor race, with a Bugatti piloted by a bloke in a crumpled cap and goggles, car

No. 12, being pursued by a rather bluer Bugatti, No. 8, round the stone balustrades along the seafront at Monaco. I turned it over before opening it and on the back, under the word Classics, was the title: *1st Monaco GP 1929 won by Williams, No. 12 Bugatti*.

The painter was named as Michael Watson FRSA FLSD. The publisher was the Parnassus Gallery, Gloucester.

I smiled, opened the card, and read, under the inscription 'To Wish You A Very Happy Birthday', the scrawl beneath:

I know it isn't but I thought you'd like this all the same. I've got something good for you – work it out for yourself. Call me to say when you can come and I'll give you some poofy tea.

It was signed *'Sergeant' Murphy* in even worse scrawl, which puzzled me. I'd never heard of Ted Murphy having a rank, not even in nickname. I pondered over the reference for a moment but soon gave up; my mind wasn't in a state to deal with conundrums and it would be easier to have Ted explain. The thought brightened me. Jeremy's desire to acquire paintings of horses wholesale was not my idea of running a discerning Art Fund; I would far rather buy individual things from cognoscenti like Ted Murphy. But then, I'm not a horse racing man; a few years ago an Indian palm reader in the Nathan Road, Hong Kong, took one look at my hand and told me never to gamble. I accepted his advice, which was like all good advice; if you can keep to it, you didn't need it in the first place.

I picked up the phone, dialled, and listened to the ringing tone. After four rings there was the click and hum of Ted's ancient answerphone swinging into action like a strouger terminal in an old Hitchcock film; dials whirred and I could imagine little mechanical arms clocking themselves round into sockets.

'This is Ted Murphy,' the answerphone's voice warbled in its own watery imitation of Ted. 'Sorry I'm not here right now. Please leave a message after the little bleep and I'll get back to you very soon.'

More hummings, a hissing silence, then a faint bleep.

'Ted,' I said, then had to harrumph to clear my sandy throat, 'this is me, Tim Simpson. Thanks for the birthday card, only four months late. I hope it's about Yvonne Aubicq. Grover looks pretty good in the Bugatti. I'll look forward to seeing an Orpsie Boy as soon as you're back, will I? It's no good asking you to get some proper tea. Why sergeant, by the way? Cheers.'

16

I put the phone down, feeling baulked. A visit to Ted Murphy's shop and gallery would have given me an excuse to go out, might have cheered me up. As it was, I'd have to obey Jeremy.

Sighing, I picked up the phone.

If I'd known then that Ted was dead already, I certainly wouldn't have bothered.

CHAPTER 3

'The body in the library,' Sue said, 'was that of a moderately well-dressed man in his mid-thirties who was clearly suffering from symptoms of alcoholic withdrawal.'

'Oh dear,' I said.

Standing in front of the large bookcase in our flat in Onslow Gardens, I avoided her cool blue eyes and downed about a quarter of a pint of cold lager whilst looking blearily and haphazardly at the spines of the books.

'At some point,' she continued remorselessly, 'the cadaver had sustained a flesh wound to the shin which had bled – noticeably – on to the expensive cover of the sofa.'

'Oh dear,' I said.

Ted Murphy hadn't phoned me back all day.

'Whatever caused the wound had also torn the dress trouser-leg of the dinner suit worn by the corpse.'

'Um, yes, oh dear, I suppose it had.'

The lager was starting to make me feel better. I drank some more of it. I'm a bitter man, naturally; lager is for medicinal purposes, when you don't want a taste to intrude.

'Were it not for the fact that the body, doubtless due to the effect of alcoholic dehydration, had started to snore *louder than a diesel engine*, concern might have been felt for its well-being.'

'Oh dear,' I said. 'Oh dear, oh dear.'

'As it was, the thoroughly wakened but devoted library staff dressed the loudly-snoring cadaver's wounds and tried to get back to its disturbed sleep. The staff's sleep, I mean, not the cadaver's. I think.'

'I'm very sorry,' I said. 'I am most grateful for the bandage. Very soothing.'

'Thank goodness that's a loose cover on the sofa. It'll have to be dry-cleaned.'

'Oh dear,' I said.

The lager was moving the blood around into veins which had not been irrigated for hours. I was glad I'd come home relatively early.

She turned her steady gaze away from me for a moment, took in the large bunch of flowers I had placed on the dining table and then looked back at me. 'Stop saying, oh dear, over and over again and tell me what on earth you got up to,' she commanded. 'Gillian says that Nobby has had to stay in bed all day.'

'I'm not surprised. Those Limehouse places must be dreadful; catch me going near them.'

Her eyes widened. 'Limehouse? He says it was all your fault.'

'All my fault? My fault? I like that! There's gratitude for you! That's typical, that is. I take good care of him until he goes careering off with a crowd of drunken rozzers in a Black Maria and then he tries to put the blame for subsequent events on me! They were bent on total mischief, all of them. Like a swarm of berserk bluebottles. We, on the other hand, were merely indulging in a harmless bit of fun with a rugby ball. Seldom are men so innocently occupied as when in sporting –'

'He says that if you hadn't attracted the attention of squads of police from Bow Street, he wouldn't have ended up in Limehouse at all. He hadn't intended to leave the dinner. It was you and Dickie Bulverhythe who initiated the whole disgraceful Waterloo Bridge business. A bet of some sort with those dreadful men from Yorkshire. The Sattersthwaites, wasn't it? I remember meeting them years ago; trouble, I thought, real trouble, both of you.'

I gave her a stern look. 'So you know the full story already. There is no need for explanations from me. You've been on the blower to Gillian Roberts for half the day, haven't you?'

Her blue eyes regarded me humorously. 'You surely didn't think Gillian wouldn't call me to find out what on earth happened, did you? She says Nobby got back after the milkman this morning and that he hasn't arrived home in that condition since they were engaged. She had to lie to the children that he'd been called out on a case and was ill. He's been in wretched shape all day, apparently. Completely recumbent and in a filthy temper.'

'Serve him right. My fault, indeed.'

'I'm rather surprised you managed to get yourself off to work.'

'Me? Why? I was just a bit overtired last night, that's all. Didn't want to disturb you so I stretched out on the sofa. Perfectly OK this morning.'

'Tim! I had to half-undress you and put a rug on you. You were blotto! You reeked! Absolutely reeked! When I left this morning I thought you'd be comatose all day.'

'Bad champagne. Always a mistake; would have been perfectly all right otherwise.'

A suspicious look came into her face. 'Where did you drink bad champagne?'

'Soho. Club of some sort. Dickie and the Sattersthwaites' idea. To settle the bet thing amicably. Would have been poor form to refuse.'

'Of course.' Her voice was not dry so much as arid. 'I know only too well how you hate letting your friends down. And a man's honour would have been involved, of course, over the bet.' She shook her head sadly. 'Am I to expect a yearly repetition of these events?'

'Oh no, no, no! You know me. Only go once every three or four years. Terrible bore to go every year; I'm not that type at all.'

'And I suppose you didn't care for all those naked ladies at the Soho club?'

'What naked ladies?'

She chuckled suddenly. 'I must say it's a change for Nobby to outdo you and the others at one of those thrashes. Gillian is quite put out.'

'Do him good. Nobby's far too uptight most of the time. To be fair, he scored a tremendous success yesterday and got a real gang leader locked up for the duration. This man Banks was the result of years of work, or something. So he was out to celebrate. Deservedly, poor chap.'

'Whereas for you it was just another reunion.'

I winced as I looked back at the bookcase. Sue takes a tolerant view of the occasional reunions I attend, reasoning that a man has to be let out occasionally, like a dog to a rat hunt, otherwise he'll get irritable and scratchy. During the not many years that we've been married, it has not been reunion dinners that have caused what strife has come up.

'What are you peering at the bookcase like that for? Have you lost something?'

'No,' I said, casually. 'I'm just wondering where that book on Munnings has got to.'

'Munnings? You mean that book of Stanley Booth's on Munnings?' Her voice registered on to a different note. Sue works at the Tate Gallery, where she is a curator specializing in the Impressionists, but inevitably British art occupies a lot of her attention. 'What do you want to find the Munnings book for? The Fund isn't going to buy a Munnings, is it?'

Munnings is not one of Sue's favourite subjects. Sir Alfred Munnings had views on modern art which, if generally accepted, would have put public taste back about fifty years. And, while he was President of the Royal Academy, shrank not from expressing them. At the top of his voice.

'Not just a Munnings, Sue. Possibly bulk quantities of them. Jeremy wants me to look at the Crockingham Collection.'

'*The Crockingham Collection?*' she nearly shouted. 'Good God, Tim, you're not going to buy anything from the Crockingham Collection are you?'

'No, not just anything, Sue. More like, say, the whole bang shoot of it.'

Her jaw dropped open.

'Sporting art,' she whispered, as though saying something nasty in church. 'Oh, no. It hasn't come to this. Surely not?'

'Jeremy is very keen on it. I believe, actually, that there's a Stubbs in the Collection, too. Not a great one, but a Stubbs is always a Stubbs.'

'Horses,' she nearly snorted.

'Horses are as good a subject as still lives and landscapes. Not as good as nudes, of course, but still very popular, Sue.'

'Jorrocks.'

'I beg your pardon? The horse is a great social emblem in British society. There's money in horses. And, by implication, in horse paintings.'

'It's disgraceful. You haven't got a Ben Nicholson in the whole Fund and yet you're going to look at those wretched daubs.'

'Jeremy doesn't like Ben Nicholson. Abstract art turns him right off. He says the one thing he cannot stand is white squares punctuated by white triangles and white circles with a dot here and there. Won't buy anything he doesn't understand, you see.'

I swallowed the last of the lager and felt a blessed sense of relief. 'I wonder if he knows what Munnings said about Francis Bacon? Quite unprintable, it was, apparently.'

She made a sound that was a cross between a cat spitting and a tiger snarling. I looked at her fondly. Finishing the lager reminded me that the world was not going to end and that I needed sustenance, badly.

'How about nipping out for a meat dhansak?' I asked. 'I can never get rid of a hangover completely until I've been to a curry house. Cholesterol's just the thing for it. As well as for the other.'

She gave me a haughty stare.

'After last night it'll take more than a bunch of flowers and a cheap curry to get me involved in the other,' she said. 'Especially if you're going to start getting all horsy.'

Mockingly, I put on a surprised look.

'I thought you were a Jilly Cooper fan,' I grinned.

This time it was what *she* said that was unprintable. Munnings would have been proud of her.

CHAPTER 4

Breakfast in Onslow Gardens, when there haven't been any rugby reunion dinners, is a peaceful affair conducted at a little table overlooking the greenery in the square outside. The next morning, I was feeling completely recovered. My tea and Sue's coffee were being consumed in a cordial atmosphere as I read *The Times* and she perused an exhibition catalogue. Our flat has suited us well for quite a time now, even though our differing tastes in art jostle slightly for position on the walls. Where I have a still life by Alan Gwynne-Jones and a sketch of a soldier by Orpen, she has a Hockney print; where I have hung an etching of Dorelia by Augustus John, she has a Picasso print of a geometrically dismembered woman. Even though she hasn't yet managed to oust my large marine oil by Clarkson Stanfield over the fireplace, she has hung her Stanley Spencer water-colour of a suburban angel with washing-line and her Sylvia Gosse still life and her Laura Knight and Dod Proctor and Elizabeth Stanhope Forbes in positions prominent enough to give the ladies more than their fair share of wall space. She has even hung her Ethel Walker interior right next to my airy Wilson Steer watercolour of the harbour at Bosham. This doesn't bother me at all; the contrasting scenes go surprisingly well together, perhaps a bit like us, and I like the work of all those artists. So domestic harmony, which reigned that morning, is not disturbed.

The ring of the doorbell spoilt all that.

Sue got up because she was nearest and went to answer. Across the little entrance hall, her expression of surprise and pleasure was tempered with a sudden note of caution. A lean, ginger-haired man with a set expression came quickly past her and crossed the carpet to stand over me at the table. Behind him, a dark, solid-looking fellow trailed respectfully through the doorway. I stared at the arrivals briefly, then sang softly but audibly to the famous melody:

> ' "In Limehouse
> Where chief inspectors love to play
> In Limehouse" – '

'Cut it out, Tim.'

The voice was sharp. Unusually, it lacked the exasperation I expect when Nobby Roberts feels baited. The tone was unmistakably serious. Sue closed the door and came to the table with an alarmed look about her. She knows Nobby well and can read his face very accurately; she gave me a faint shake of the head in warning.

I noticed that the ginger hair was bristled and unkempt. His clothes were creased. He is normally very careful about his appearance and this first surprised, then chilled me. Surely his hangover couldn't have lasted that long? I cut back the bantering greeting I had been about to bring forth; suddenly he looked too official.

'What's up?'

His freckled face and pinkish eyes looked worriedly down at me.

'A man called Ted Murphy. A dealer. Did you know him, Tim?'

I looked past Nobby at the dark, solid man who stood looking at me without expression. He would be a sergeant, I guessed. He was too watchful for comfort; Nobby seemed very conscious of his presence.

The use of the past tense had made the blood drain from my face.

'Did I know? You mean do I, don't you? Of course I know Ted Murphy. Antiques and paintings. Shop and gallery in the Fulham Road.'

'I'm sorry, Tim. Bad news, I'm afraid. He's dead.'

'Dead?'

'This is Sergeant Cook of Chelsea CID.' Nobby gestured at the other man, who nodded at me. 'He is part of the investigating team. Sergeant, this is Tim Simpson. And his wife, Sue – er – Mrs Simpson.'

The sergeant came forward, shook hands with both of us,

pronouncing a respectful Sir and Madam, then looked back expectantly at Nobby. I was still floundering.

'*Dead?* Ted Murphy?'

I couldn't get the hang of this. Nobby was absolutely serious; this was no clever joke. Sue was staring at me now, with a look I've seen too often before. Not a look I like.

'Sergeant Cook will give you the details.' Nobby was deadpan, revealing nothing. 'There are some questions he'd like to ask you. He'll *have* to ask you.'

'Just a minute.' I found I had to clear my throat. 'This means there was foul play, does it? You two being here, I mean?'

'I'm afraid so, sir.' The sergeant's voice was deep but clear. 'Mr Murphy was murdered. There is no doubt of that. I am making inquiries in order to find his killer and apprehend him, or her, or them, as the case may be.'

'Murdered?' Incredulity made my voice hoarse again.

'Yes, sir. Murphy was shot dead as he got out of his car in the early hours of yesterday morning. He was found some hours after the shooting, in the back alley where he parked, lying beside his car.'

'Good God!'

'I'll get you both some coffee.' Sue's voice was very quiet. She picked up the coffee pot and disappeared into the kitchenette, leaving the two policemen staring at me after they'd thanked her.

'Sit down, for heaven's sake.'

They sat, turning their chairs to face me. I looked into my congealing tea cup, slowly going into shock. Ted Murphy had been a quiet, slim, soberly-dressed man in his forties; a semi-friend from the days way back when I, too, lived in the Fulham Road and racketed about in bachelor abandon. He had one of those shops that you can sometimes call a gallery, sometimes a shop; you're never quite sure which. I suppose that defines an unsuccessful dealer. He mixed paintings with furniture and bric-à-brac in a way that sometimes had great style and sometimes failed completely; the sort of activity in which you could hardly fail to make money ten years ago, but which is now dying so fast that the lush lily-pool of dealers, drained by auctioneers, resembles an empty millpond in which old mussels wallow dying in wet mud. From time to time, I'd drop in for a chat and he'd tell me how terrible trade was these days, not like old times

25

at all, smoking interminable Benson & Hedges cigarettes as he looked round irritably at his stock, with flicking, critical eyes. He talked well, as you might expect from a Murphy, and I liked his self-deprecating humour a lot; we both had the same, quirky, biographical fascination with the artists of the modern period – that means art from anything after about 1860 up to 1950 or so, after which it's called contemporary. Ted had been to art school before he took up dealing and was English-Irish, if you know what I mean. If you don't, it's too hard to explain to an outsider.

Now he was dead.

'In checking through his flat above the shop,' Sergeant Cook's deep rumble was still very clear, 'we listened to his telephone answering machine. Rather an ancient old unit, but it worked. The last message on it was from a Tim Simpson, yesterday. Was that you, sir?'

'Yes, it was.' As the initial shock faded, a hole, a deep hole like a missing tooth, was opening up in my mind.

He made a note in a little book. 'Thank you, sir. We ran a check on the name and, especially in connection with the art trade, our computer records had quite an entry.'

'Did they really?'

Gap syndrome, that was it. A sudden onslaught of mind-related gap syndrome was numbing my response.

'Oh, yes. Quite a long entry. It also had a "refer to DCI Roberts at Scotland Yard" notation to it. So we did, yesterday evening. The chief inspector here naturally advised us on your – your situation, and we agreed it would be most helpful if he was to be involved. So that's how it comes about that we are here, first thing today, you might say.'

'I see.'

'I'm sorry if this has been a shock to you, sir, but you'll appreciate that time is of the essence in this sort of case.'

'Of course. But it has.'

An empty space is contrary to nature. The gap was starting to ache around its edges.

'Do you feel able to answer questions?'

'Fire away.'

It was an inappropriate response, just unthinking, but I decided to leave it. Cook gave me an odd look then continued.

'May I first of all ask you, sir, where you were the night before last?'

I took my eyes off the table and looked at Nobby. His face was absolutely expressionless.

'Certainly. I was at a rugby club reunion dinner at the Savoy Grill. Detective Chief Inspector Roberts was my guest.'

'Thank you, sir. That confirms what the chief inspector has told me. I gather you separated after the meal. At about midnight. Did you then return here?'

'Er, no. I went to Soho with some friends from the dinner. To a club.'

'What club was that, sir?'

'I'm afraid that the name escapes me. But perhaps my friends, whose guest I was, could tell you.'

'I see, sir. May I ask what time you came home?'

I swallowed, but Sue's voice cut in.

'I can tell you, because he woke me up.' She put their coffees down on the table. 'It was just after three.'

'Thank you, madam. And you didn't leave the house after that?'

'No, I didn't. Not until the next morning, when I went to work at about nine-thirty.'

'Thank you.' Cook took a swig of his coffee. 'Very kind, madam, thank you.' He turned back to me. 'Had you known Mr Murphy long?'

'Quite a few years. Not intimately. I used to live near there, in the Fulham Road. Then he and I kept in contact because of a mutual liking for modern British art. I am the administrator of an art investment fund, and I bought a number of paintings through him. Either from him directly or as a result of information from him, for which he was paid a fee.'

'I see, sir. So he was a sort of runner for you?'

'Er, yes, I suppose you could say that.' Ted wouldn't have liked the description; he wouldn't have liked it at all.

'And when did you last see him?'

I had to think. 'Quite a long time ago. Ah, yes, at the Sickert exhibition at the Royal Academy. That must have been January.'

'But you have spoken to him since?'

'On the phone a few times, sure.'

The sergeant was making notes. He stopped, pulled out a

27

piece of paper, and looked up at me. 'The message you left on the answering machine; is this a correct transcription of it?'

He handed me the piece of paper and I read it, with its odd notes on spelling. The message had been carefully broken down into sentences of a sort.

Ted, this is me, Tim Simpson.

Thanks for the birthday card, only four months late.

I hope it's about Yvonne Aubeak (Orbeek?)

Grover (Groover?) looks pretty good in the Bugatti.

I'll look forward to seeing an Orpsy Boy (Aupsea Bhoy?) as soon as you're back, will I?

It's no good asking you to get some proper tea.

Why sergeant, by the way? Cheers.

I nodded briefly, finding it hard to speak. It read very oddly. Almost suggestively. The last message on Ted's answerphone, and he had never heard it. When I was sitting in my office mouthing it, he was already down on a slab somewhere, finding out what happens after the last move. If anything. It was probably while I was taxi-ing home from my night out, full of bibulous bonhomie, that someone had ended it all for him.

Prematurely.

Nobby took the paper from me and looked at it. I guessed it wasn't the first time he'd seen it, but a slight frown came to his eyebrows as though he was trying to decipher it afresh.

'I wonder,' Sergeant Cook said, 'if you would mind just running through the message for me, so we can understand it.' He accepted the paper from Nobby, who glanced at Sue and then at him with a sort of apprehension in his face. 'If you'd rather not, at this stage, we could perhaps postpone it until later.'

He looked at me intently as he said this, as though expecting me to put off the event. Nobby's face betrayed further tension. I thought for a fleeting moment that they were thinking of my feelings over Ted, then realized that the coded reference to Yvonne Aubicq was what might be causing them to be over-tactful in front of my wife. Or even, perhaps, in Cook's case, mention of an Orpsie Boy. Or a Groover in a Bugatti; it could sound very suggestive. Sensitive fellows; I smiled slightly and said no, it's OK, I can do it now. That seemed to make them relax a bit.

The sergeant looked at the paper and read it out, slowly.

'"Ted, this is me, Tim Simpson". That's simple enough. Then

"thanks for the birthday card, only four months late".' He looked up. 'Can you explain that? He sent you a card or an illustration of some sort, did he?'

I got up, went across to my briefcase on the other side of the room and found the card where I'd put it on leaving the office. The envelope wasn't with it, so I must have discarded it somewhere. I put the card down on the table in front of them, seeing with new eyes the pale blue surround and the two Bugattis against the sandy-balustraded background of Monaco, gaily-coloured flags flying. Number 12 sped towards me, its goggled and cloth-capped driver leaning with his elbow over the side of the car, ready to take the next bend, frozen in speed forever.

Sergeant Cook picked it up gingerly, as though expecting something distasteful. A sort of relief spread across his face as he put it in front of Nobby, on the table between them.

They opened it up, read the inscription, turned it over, and read the title: *1st Monaco GP 1929 won by Williams No. 12 Bugatti.*

'That came yesterday,' I told them. 'My call to Ted Murphy was in response to it.'

Cook took the card and opened it again. He read the writing out loud.

'I know it isn't but I thought you'd like this all the same. I've got something good for you – work it out for yourself. Call me to say when you can come and have some poofy tea. "Sergeant" Murphy.'

He frowned. 'Sergeant? Was Murphy in the army or something, once?'

'Not to my knowledge. Let me explain the rest, though.'

I got up slowly and stretched, deciding where to begin. It was all quite logical to me and Ted, except the sergeant part, but what it would sound like to them was another matter.

'The card is a commercial birthday card that Ted bought in a shop somewhere. The illustration is the key. It shows the English driver Williams winning the 1929 Monaco Grand Prix in a Bugatti. That is an historical fact known, I imagine, to historical racing enthusiasts. He was a works driver for Bugatti, particularly on the Paris circuits, but his name wasn't really Williams.' I smiled as they looked up from the card. 'Originally it was Grover; William Charles Frederick Grover. That was when he was the Rolls chauffeur to Sir William Orpen, the famous portrait painter and RA. Hence my remark about Grover looks pretty good in the Bugatti. Orpen was a terrific artist; he's a bit of an obsession of mine, and was for Ted, too. The Anglo-Irish connection, you see; Orpen came from Dublin Protestants like Ted. That was what he told me, anyway. Unusual for a Murphy perhaps, but there it is. Was.'

Nobby leant forward. 'So Murphy was hinting, or even telling you outright, that he had found an Orpen somewhere?'

'Well done, Nobby. But possibly more than that. Straightforward Orpens are not that rare and his portraits are all over. But during the First World War he was an official war artist. He took up with a beautiful French girl from Lille called Yvonne Aubicq; a blonde. Fell for her like a ton of bricks; everyone got to know that Orpen – Orpsie Boy as he called himself – was besotted by his new mistress. His paintings of her are really special. A famous one of her nude in bed, called "Early Morning" went for over £300,000 back in May 1990 when things were booming. The next – in November of that year, called "The Disappointing Letter" – somewhat similar – was bought in. Didn't reach its reserve. The collapse was on and the money wasn't there. But another painting of Yvonne Aubicq is something I've always wanted to buy for the Art Fund. At a decent price, of course. I bought a studio self-portrait by Orpen, with her nude on a couch, mirrored, at Christerby's a few years back for £26,000 plus. Ted always admired that purchase. I hoped the Williams card was telling me he'd found another. That's what I meant by, "I hope it's about Yvonne Aubicq."'

Yvonne Aubicq; I had my own reasons for having that name, and that image, engraved in my memory, but I wasn't telling any policemen about that, not in front of Sue. Married men have to let their previous lives die quiet, like old ghosts finally wreathed into evaporation.

Cook looked relieved for some reason, but also slightly bemused. 'I'm not quite with you,' he said. 'What was the significance of Williams or Grover – in relation to this Yvonne girl?'

I saw a slight smile come to Sue's face for the first time since the arrival of the force. She's always liked the story, too. Not surprisingly; it's one of the most romantic bits of real biography you can get. The problem for me has always been its other connotations; the things that I never mention to Sue.

'Orpen was something of a ladies' man. His wife and family were quite used to it. Some time round 1928, he dropped

30

Yvonne in favour of another lady. Something I've never understood because everyone who knew Yvonne said how super she was, beautiful, but sweet and unaffected. Not the mistress image at all. Anyway, he was generous to her and gave her a small wooden house near Paris and money. He also gave her his Rolls-Royce. In those days, the chauffeur went with the car like the tyres or the steering wheel. So Grover went to France with Yvonne. He changed his name to Grover-Williams, raced Bugattis for the official team, and he married her. It must have been a great life. Until the Second World War they were marvellously happy.'

'Good Lord!' said Sergeant Cook.

'So I hoped the painting Ted had found would be to do with Yvonne Aubicq. She and Grover-Williams were married in 1929. The poofy tea bit was a reference to Ted liking China tea. He always drank it. That perfumed stuff doesn't go with a rugby-playing image; I used to pull his leg about it being effeminate. That's all that's about.'

Cook stared down at his notebook. He was dressed in a grey suit and striped shirt with a dark tie. I put him down as about my own age, equally stocky. He can't have been all that delighted to find himself landed with a Scotland Yard DCI breathing down his neck, especially one so closely connected with the Art Fraud Squad. He seemed fairly imperturbable, though my story must have taken a bit of absorbing and the notebook had a lot of marks on it. I wondered what he had been expecting when he came to see me. Ted and I had always used that sort of shorthand about art: odd references to places, people, background things – just to test each other. The card was a clever message. It probably seemed ridiculous to outsiders.

'The only thing you haven't explained,' Nobby said, 'is the "sergeant" bit.'

'I know. I don't understand that at all. I once had a problem with sergeant and Sargent' – I glanced quickly at Sue – 'but the painter John S. Sargent has nothing to do with this. I expect Ted intended to explain it all when we met. Some witty allusion of his, no doubt.'

'I see,' Cook said, as though he didn't see at all. 'You were on pretty close terms with Murphy, though, by the sound of it.'

'At this sort of level, yes, I was. People in the art trade like the

31

sort of work-speak you've found here. They have close working relationships like people in any industry, without necessarily having much personal knowledge. I know nothing about Ted's private life. He didn't have a wife that I ever saw, for instance.'

I paused at that point, hearing myself speaking with a deliberately casual tone, as a man might do while lying. I wasn't lying, strictly speaking: it was absolutely true that I'd never seen Ted with a wife, or even a girlfriend. We always met in masculine circumstances, over a beer or at his shop. But Ted, I was sure, was a man whose life in that respect was reprehensibly clandestine; there were lady friends about somewhere, women he just hinted at, possibly adulterous liaisons. A man does not reach an age of over forty, apparently unmarried, without having something to hide. Ted knew that I was firmly married, that Sue and I, even after normal ructions, were a fixture. He didn't trespass on that knowledge. In the same way, he didn't volunteer personal information to me, never boasted or presented a new conquest. He had an almost continental discretion. Such things were not part of our relationship.

'Pity,' Cook said, still looking a bit puzzled. 'It might have helped to know a bit more about that side of him.'

I shrugged. 'Sorry. Can't help you there. He talked well, was very funny sometimes, and kept his figure. But outside of his shop and an odd drink in a pub, that was it. I never saw him in a domestic context. Didn't know him that well. Just art and China tea, really.'

China tea; the association made me glance at Nobby, setting the melody off again.

'Oh Limehouse kid
Oh oh oh Limehouse kid
Going the way that the rest of them did—'

I kept it to myself and tried to resettle my mind round the hole that throbbed there. No Ted Murphy; no more any Ted Murphy. On you go, with another one less to talk to.

Sergeant Cook was looking at his notes thoughtfully. After a short pause, he looked at me directly and said: 'You say that between midnight and three, when you got back here, you were at this, er, this nightclub?'

'Yes, I was.'

'Can you substantiate that?'

'Certainly. I was with three friends.'

He nodded reassuringly. 'I may have to ask you for their details.'

'No problem.'

He nodded again and looked back at his notes. Sue had a soft expression on her face, keeping me in view, but Nobby had started to tap his fingers on the table top. That's always a bad sign.

'It's extraordinary!' he suddenly burst out, making Cook look up in surprise.

'What?' I demanded.

'You. And things like this. You only have to get a card from an art dealer you know quite superficially and in no time the poor bugger's dead.'

'Thank you very much! Nobby, I don't think —'

'No! Don't deny it! It's happened so often! When they phoned me from Chelsea, I groaned out loud. I've got more work than I can handle and once again you've started swanning about with mayhem in attendance.'

I gaped at him before sarcasm started to well up irresistibly within me.

'Well. I'm sorry to be a burden to you, I must say, Nobby. Extremely sorry. Naturally, if I'd known my extremely peripheral involvement was going to put you out like this and interrupt your extremely important work, I'd never have made my phone call. The Art Fund could go hang. I'm sure Ted Murphy would have avoided giving you problems, too. In future, I'll —'

'Peripheral involvement it is!' he interrupted. 'Extremely peripheral. And solely peripheral. Don't get any strange notions that you have a role to play in this! The murder is probably a domestic matter. Most of them are.'

'Well, in that case why are you getting so distraught about my telephone call? Domestic, you say; Ted had a wife, had he?'

He scowled. 'Apparently not.'

'Girlfriend?'

'We are investigating several possibilities.'

'Several? Lucky fellow. How was he killed? What sort of gun?'

33

'Shotgun blast,' Cook said, now looking up alertly from his notes. 'Close range. Nasty.'

I shook my head. 'Not a girlfriend's method, that. Not usually. More like a –'

'*Stop!*' Nobby shot to his feet. 'Stop this! Right now!' He gestured to Cook. 'Come on. We're leaving. There's quite enough to be going on with. You are not to give him any further details. You may question him as much as you like, and doubtless you'll think of other questions in due course. But under no circumstances – absolutely none – is Mr Simpson to become involved in this inquiry. You hear me? You heard that, too, Tim? No involvement. Am I making myself clear?'

I stared up at him. 'Really, Nobby. You must calm yourself. You're going all pink. What involvement? Ted Murphy wasn't a close friend. I didn't know him that well. It's not a question of my seeking to avenge him or anything.'

'I know that. It doesn't have to be, with you. All you need is a mystery and a painting to go after. Your track record is as well-beaten as a motorway.' He held up a finger. 'Let me warn you, Tim. Leave this alone. Well alone. We will take a very dim view of any amateur sleuthing. Got it?'

'Of course I've got it, Nobby. I can't imagine why you're getting so het up.'

He glared at me. I knew what he was thinking. The leopard never changes its spots. People never alter. To change people you have to screw electrodes into their skulls and burn out quantities of the little grey cells inside.

'Damn!' he nearly shouted. 'Damn, damn, *damn*! I have bad vibes about this! Really bad vibes! Come on, Will. No more information, or he'll never leave you alone.'

They left in a rush. So Sergeant Cook's name was Will. You always learn something on these occasions.

Sue came back from closing the door and stared at me.

'What is it?' I asked.

'Come on, Tim. You know what I'm thinking.'

I spread my hands. 'I've got nothing to hide. Nothing. Poor bloody old Ted. It hurts, but it's nothing to do with me. Besides, I'm much too busy. I have to go to Suffolk to see the blasted Crockingham Collection. That puts quite enough horseplay on my plate for the moment.'

Sue compressed her lips. Her eyes narrowed. Then they went

out to our big bookcase, back to me, round the room, then back to me again. I looked back at her innocently.

An empty space is contrary to nature. This one, reacting to the immediate extraction, was starting to ache quite badly.

Sue got up and reached for her handbag.

'I shall be coming with you,' she announced.

CHAPTER 5

The county of Suffolk is still very rural despite determined attempts to change it. At its southern boundary you have Essex, enough said, where sub-Cockneyland spreads its teeless speech and too-smart tentacles steadily northwards. To the county's coast along the North Sea, rumble convoys of container lorries with goods for the Continental ports in increasing tonnages via Felixstowe and Harwich, shaking the thatched roadside cottages to the base of their timbers. The northern half, however, towards Norfolk, can still claim to belong to an imaginary country existence that was never real, where harsh agricultural realities get blurred in memory-mists of fond harvesting and fruity produce which, in recollection, do not seem to have required the bone-cracking effort that really brought them about.

It is nothing like it was when Alfred Munnings was born, a hundred and fifteen years ago, the second son of a country miller at Mendham, on the Suffolk bank of the river Waveney. From that white weather-boarded mill with its integral house, set amongst low water meadows and splashy reeded surfaces, sparkling ripples of light and the shadows of tall feathery trees, to which teams of garlanded wagons drawn by huge farm horses brought the scythed harvest for grinding, he set out on an artist's life in Norwich, Paris and London. Horses, dogs and the steady rhythm of rural life, home-brewed beer, vast game dishes and coarse-grained sturdy men who could play the piano, sing and recite after a hard day's work, provided the basis of his culture, along with painting, books and poetry. He thought that the invention of the wireless was a disaster. He drank port to gouty excess. He was no intellectual, no abstract imaginer. It was Munnings who said that if he ever met Picasso, he'd kick Picasso where he deserved it, straight up the arse.

Crockingham Hall lay to the north of the county, between

Stowmarket and Diss, off the main roads and down twisted lanes with missing hedges bordering open fields. Clumps of trees broke the rolling smoothness of crop-filled land, waving with short incipient corn or sprouted green with hundreds of acres of chard and that feeble spinach you get in supermarkets, packed in clear plastic bags, together with the inseparable grit that gets in your teeth. Church spires were frequent. In the hamlets, old thatched or pantiled houses, some of them with jettied upper storeys, leant confidentially towards the road. You'll have guessed that I'm an urban man, not addicted to watching the rain pelting on to ploughed fields, but I had to agree that the villages presented an idyllic image. The car rolled past pink-washed walls, pargeting and front gardens in which hollyhocks, foxgloves and the like mingled with enormous local cabbages, cultivated mainly for boot and shoe repairs.

Sue hummed gently to herself while I concentrated on keeping the Jaguar's side from being peeled by passing agricultural implements bristling with spikes. The local clay has engendered tractor-drawn machinery of a particularly medieval appearance, like an arras or *chevaux de frise* intended to puncture powerful besieging cavalry.

'Have you met Philip Carberry?' she demanded, suddenly breaking a reverie and turning towards me with a probing expression.

'Yes, once or twice. With Jeremy, of course.'

'Are they close friends?'

'I wouldn't say that. Acquainted in more than one direction – yachting and investments – but not really close. Philip Carberry is one of Jeremy's many contacts. Actually, the father – Sir Andrew Carberry – is an old contact of Sir Richard White's, so the thing goes back a long way. I got the impression from Sir Richard that he views Sir Andrew Carberry as something of an eccentric survival. Sort of Squire Weston with art-collecting instincts. Knight of the shires, stalwart of the Tory Party, was an MP once, but there was a bit of a hoo-ha about a business conflict of interest so he stood down at the next election. Before, presumably, there were embarrassments for the Party. You know how it is.'

'Do I?'

'Perhaps not.'

I said this automatically, without conviction. Sue adopts an innocent art-loving attitude towards the business world which deceives me not at all. She is as shrewd as they come, but the image is important to her so I try not to dent it.

'Anyway,' I continued, 'the ex-MP bit is unimportant now. The Carberry family have been badly hit by the Lloyds fiasco. Somehow they seem to have an unerring instinct for duff syndicates and natural disasters. According to Jeremy, they've not done much to create wealth for some time; no less than three of them are names and their Lloyds losses in the cumulative sense are likely to deplete the coffers very considerably. The suggestion that the Collection could save them comes from Philip rather than anyone else, I gather. His father is hostile to the idea, but faced with the crunch would rather dispose of the paintings than the real thing. He still owns racehorses at Newmarket and hunts up here somewhere.'

'What about the rest of the family? Who else is there?'

'Another brother and a sister. I don't know about them.'

'With any luck,' Sue sounded sharp, 'they'll oppose the disposal bitterly.'

I grinned as we passed the village sign for Crockingham. Sue was not going to encourage me to commit the Fund to sporting art, obviously. Recently, she had been quite open in wanting to know why we hadn't bought Ben Nicholson and Victor Pasmore and a few other abstractionists. My acquisition of Tissot paintings had been met with a sad shake of the head. Even a somewhat cubist Nevinson had brought out a sympathetic smile, hinting of my elementary understanding of modern art. To point out to Sue that investment in art is something quite different from an advanced appreciation of it, only meets with an even more condescending smile and a sad shake of the head. Fortunately, she refrains from interfering as much as she can; only when driven to distraction does she take the plunge.

We were arriving at Crockingham Hall.

The building that hove into sight, down a drive lined with lime trees, was reached by crossing a moat. Moated buildings are quite common in Suffolk and are not confined to castles. Quite modest farmhouses can boast of moats around there, and quite modest farmhouses are often called halls, since that, technically and architecturally, is how they started out. But Crockingham Hall was not too modest; it was mainly timbered, with brick nogging between beams in that herringbone pattern they liked, under a tiled roof with high patterned Elizabethan chimneys. A wing going out at a right angle was plastered and washed pink, but the end gabled wall we approached was jettied out three storeys high and its brickwork was beautifully symmetrical. The effect was warm and ancient; Sue sat up in her seat.

A notice by the drive proclaimed Crockingham Hall – the Collection open to the public on Tuesdays and Saturdays only. An arrow pointed towards the plastered, pink-washed wing. Evidently this was the gallery; the house itself, with a double bank of roofs and several clusters of chimneys, was attached but conveniently separate.

I avoided the public car park and drew up in front of the house next to a Bentley saloon and a BMW on the gravel sweep. The front door opened and an English setter ran barking cheerfully round, shaking its grey-white spotted coat and grinning at me as I got out of the Jaguar. I grinned back and chucked it under the chin before patting its head, but I'd done the wrong thing; a shout called it away from me. A red-faced, white-haired old cove in a loud houndstooth sports jacket and whipcord breeches stumped down the steps as the dog ran back inside. Beetled brows scowled over blue piercing eyes that glared at me. The old cove's check flannel shirt bulged tightly on the chest and round the neck; even his shoes looked too tight.

'Gallery's round the side,' he rasped.

The voice was one it takes a lot of good food and drink, especially drink, to develop. It had a bad-tempered fruitiness that put me in mind of wasp-infested plums.

He was followed out by a younger man, my sort of age, in a grey City suit and black townee shoes with thin soles.

'Hello, Tim,' he said. Then looking at the old man, 'This is Tim Simpson from White's Bank, Father.'

'Business is business. Trade's trade,' the old cove ground out, staring at me aggressively. 'Side entrance for the gallery. That's what you're here for.'

He gave me another glare, nodded perfunctorily, stumped back in through the front door and slammed it. I stared after him, bemused. The younger man put on an apologetic expression.

'Sorry about my father. I'm afraid he's not taking things very well just at present.'

I held out my hand. 'No trouble,' I said. 'How are you, Philip?'

He was a slight fellow, rather lean, with a harassed expression emphasized by deep lines around the eyes, which were brown and slightly hooded. He looked nothing like his parent; his yachtsmanship must be keeping him nimble.

'I'm well, thanks, given the circumstances.' He shook my hand. 'It's a terrible time financially. Oh, you've got someone with you? Your assistant?'

He was staring rather worriedly into the car.

'My wife, Sue. She's come up for the ride.'

Relief straightened him up. 'Oh. Oh, of course. Sorry, it's just that we don't want anyone to – to – you know – '

'Of course not. Absolute discretion.'

'Thanks.' He sounded quite grateful. 'I should have known. I'm sure we can rely on White's for that. The curator here, who looks after the place when it's open to the public, knows nothing about your interest. I've told him you've come from White's from the insurance angle, just checking how things are arranged. So I'd be obliged if you'd say nothing in front of him.'

'Of course.'

'Well, if you'd like to come round – '

'Certainly.'

I clambered back into the car, letting him walk round the side of the house. Sue raised her eyebrows at me.

'Trade to the side entrance,' I explained, feeling definitely irritated. 'The old josser's Sir Andrew Carberry. The other is Philip, his son. Jeremy's mate. The one who started all this. His father isn't what you might call delighted by our arrival.'

'Oh.' Sue put on a slightly amused look, then composed herself. 'Been put in your place, have you?'

'You bet. I said you were just up for the ride, by the way. He was worried about the news leaking out. Mum's the word, especially in front of the curator.'

Her nose tilted upwards. 'My lips are sealed. You won't get a peep out of me. I know my place; not like some I could mention.'

'Jorrocks to you, too.'

We parked in front of the gallery door beside a pockmarked yellow Lada and an old Land Rover. This was the side for the workers, evidently. After I'd introduced Sue, Philip Carberry opened up.

'It's not a public opening day, of course, so you can have free range.' He smiled at Sue. 'Do you like art?'

'Oh, yes.' Her voice was as sweet as honey. 'I love *art.*'

The change of tone on the word 'art' didn't register with him. He nodded approvingly and we entered a high, airy, raftered and beamed room going up two storeys, with a balustraded gallery built round halfway up so that paintings could be hung on two levels. He stood back with a gesture of pride to let us take it in.

'This is part of the oldest structure of the house. All timbered. The brick nogging on the other parts came later. We opened it up to put it back almost as it was when it was originally built, but we had to alter it a bit for the light and so on. I think it was a successful adaptation. Ah, here comes Frank.'

A tallish man, around fifty, in a brown sports coat and flannels came in through an interior door. He had a badge on his lapel which gave him the appearance of a steward and he was carrying a catalogue.

'Frank Hobart,' Philip Carberry said. 'The curator of the gallery.'

We were introduced and shook hands.

'If there's any information you need,' Hobart's voice was local, or perhaps slightly Norfolk, with a singsong lilt to it, 'please do ask me. I've lived with these works of art for a long time and I'm always happy to talk about them.'

He handed me the catalogue and stood, expectant, a leathery, tough sort of man with more of an outdoor appearance than you'd expect for someone who spends his time in a gallery under artificial lighting, but then I supposed he only had to open up two days a week.

'Thanks, Frank.' Philip Carberry's tone was friendly. 'I expect Mr Simpson will want to browse round for a bit before he has any questions. I'll go and see if we can rustle up some refreshments. What can I get? Coffee?'

'Coffee would be fine.'

'Good.'

'I'll see to it, Philip.' Hobart nodded briefly at the door. 'I'll have a word with Angela.'

'Oh, thank you, Frank.'

It all seemed very straightforward and natural. Hobart briskly disappeared through the interior door and Philip Carberry

41

dropped his voice. 'We don't want to set off a strong, muscular hare or something. Get Frank all worried about nothing. If we don't, in the end, you know –'

'Of course not.'

'He's only part time, of course, but he's devoted to the place.'

'I'm sure.'

'He's worked for my father for quite a time, now. We would always keep a place for him, even if the Collection were to go. They were in the army together – Cyprus and Egypt – so my father feels particularly strongly about it. Actually, we were wondering whether your Fund couldn't keep the Collection here, as it is. It would cost no more than any other storage place, I'm sure.'

'Umm,' I murmured, distracted.

'It'd make quite a few locals happy.'

'Indeed?'

I hardly heard him. My eyes were wandering to take it all in. The paintings ranged round the walls, at ground level and in the upper gallery. Block stands for sculptures supported bronzes of horses of differing sizes. I started to recognize some of the artists: a Munnings of a horse fair with gypsies, a Lucy Kemp Welch of a brewer's dray, a John Skeaping of a race almost suggested rather than defined by its zooming modern lines, another by someone I didn't know. I opened the catalogue and began to take in the names: Lionel Edwards, J. T. E. Kenney, Holiday, 'Snaffles' Payne, Dupont. It was a new world to me.

'They're all relatively modern, of course.' Philip Carberry gestured around. 'There has to be a specialization somewhere. We haven't got any of the eighteenth- and nineteenth-century painters, except where there's a slight overlap into the twentieth. The only exception is the Stubbs. My father couldn't resist that; he bought it a long time ago.'

His gesture stopped at a small painting near us, depicting a black horse in front of a haystack, looking down rather dubiously at a spotted hound. Knowing the size of the Stubbs in the Tate, I couldn't help smiling a little at Sue, but her face showed interest and she stepped across to examine it more closely.

'That's nice. 1780s?' she queried, looking back towards Philip Carberry.

'Er, yes.' He seemed a bit surprised. 'We think so. It's not

42

actually dated but it's generally thought to be from that period. He did a lot of his famous farming scenes then.'

'Ah.'

'Of course, if we'd had one with a lion or a tiger in it we'd be into a different value altogether.'

'Indeed.'

Sue's voice was grave. She was looking dubiously at the spotted hound. I resisted the urge to smile and walked away from them, down the gallery towards the end, where a Munnings *pièce de résistance* was featured with a lot of wall to itself.

The 'Start at Newmarket'.

In my pocket, the list Penny had obligingly researched for me back at the bank had a few of Munnings's 'Starts at Newmarket' on it. They were always more expensive than the other titles in any given auction season. £140,000 and £188,000 in 1981–2. As much as £220,000 in 1983–4; that was a record for any twentieth-century British artist ever, at that time. Up to £630,000-odd in 1987–8, before the slump.

This was a striking version: the nearest jockey, up on a brown horse, wore white riding gear with red striping and a red cap. Behind him were jockeys in blue and green and harlequin colours, all struggling to hold bucking mounts that were raring to go. The sense of excitement, tension and expectancy was infectious; you felt you wished you were there, had a bet on, could shout at them.

'He always said that the start of the race was the best thing to paint.' Philip Carberry was at my elbow. 'More exciting than the finish.'

'More spectacular.' Sue's voice was neutral. 'The colours all mixed. The tension. Easier for composition, too.'

Philip Carberry smiled slightly. 'That's true. This is the best of the Munnings's we have. We have quite a few; some are sketches and so on, which you could buy for a few hundred pounds or less in the 'sixties and 'seventies, but some are more finished, like the horse fair over there. He came from Mendham, you see, which is not so very far away, and Father knew him a bit. Used to see him at Newmarket. Of course, he lived at Dedham by then, and was getting on in years. Died in 1959. We haven't got the same sort of quality that the Norwich Museum has, but we've got some nice ones. This is the showpiece.'

43

'His lithographs are marvellous.' Sue said it as a sort of statement, and I flashed a warning glance towards her.

'We haven't got any of those.' Philip Carberry sounded regret-
ful. 'He trained as a lithographer, of course, at Page's of Norwich.
It's where he learnt that fantastic accuracy of drawing. Before
his eye injury. I wish we had one. Ah, here comes Frank.'

We paused for coffee and I engaged the curator in conversation. He said he had no formal training in art, he was just a
countryman who loved paintings of horses. Due to an injury
inflicted by a combine harvester, he wasn't up to farming any
more, so he'd applied for this job to supplement his disability
pension, citing a distant horse-painting ancestor to make the
point that equestrian art ran in the family. He seemed a very
decent, genuine sort; very keen on Munnings and Dupont, both
of whom were relatively local. His appearance was deceptive; I
realized that he must be older than he looked and had kept
himself in good condition, despite the injury, whatever it was.
If he and Sir Andrew Carberry were in Cyprus and Egypt
together – presumably as officer and other rank – that put them
both possibly somewhere in their sixties.

Afterwards, I did the full tour of the gallery, pausing to consult
the catalogue from time to time. The experience was a bit stultifying. In the past, I had bought most of the Fund's paintings
one at a time, convincing myself that this or that canvas was one
we should go for; building myself up to the point of purchase or
bid at auction with information and emotion in order to be
convincing. Art investment, like art collecting, is all a question of
illusion, of image. You could argue the same of many companies
when.it comes to valuing their brand names, their so-called
good will, but at least with companies there is, at the end of it all,
an asset value which relates to something tangible or saleable on
a market which has a statistical, not a fashionable, basis. Despite
Sue's dislike, paintings of horses, like racehorses themselves,
are usually bought by those more impervious to fashion than
the general run of collectors. Munnings might not be attracting
big money right now, but who could say what would happen
when a well-provenanced, really good one was put up on the
market?

I hadn't always bought one painting at a time, though; I once
acquired three Tissots together privately, and I'd several times
bought more than one painting in the same auction. I went

round, trying to keep my mind open, thinking of Jeremy and the piercing questions I might have to face. But somehow my concentration began to fade. The repetition of horses, particularly racehorse portraits, began to make me feel jaded. After a while, the subject palled. They were like portraits of any kind; either you have to have some connection with the sitter or they have to be bloody brilliant to grab your attention. The bronzes left me cold, even one by Skeaping which I could see was superb. There were one or two paintings of a hunt in full cry which stirred my blood, and the Munnings horse fair and New-market scene and one of Canadian cavalry, but after a while the only adjective I could think of was stultifying. The collector of this assemblage lacked an eye, that was it; the Collection was a safe sort of work, without flair. It was to do with quantity rather than quality. I began to leaf through the catalogue to identify the pieces as Sue walked round behind me, taking longer than I did. Her face gave nothing away.

We finished our careful perusal. I found Frank Hobart standing at my elbow.

'What do you think of it all?' he queried.

'Very interesting. An amazing collection.'

'I'm glad. Sir Andrew has taken enormous trouble over it. Years of enthusiasm and acquisition. We're very proud to have it here.'

'I'm sure you are.' I held the catalogue up for him to see. 'Is this the complete catalogue?'

'Oh, yes.' He gestured at the walls. 'It's all in there.'

'You mean there are no other works at all, anywhere here at Crockingham, or elsewhere, that belong in the Collection?'

His look wavered slightly. 'No, I'm pretty sure that all the relevant works are there. A few drawings and sketches and so on are not in the catalogue — we only put in the things that are on show — but the proper Collection is fully itemized.'

'Good. As long as I have the complete list.'

'I understand.' He nodded, watching me warily.

I put the catalogue carefully in my pocket before thanking him and going outside to the car, accompanied by Sue and Philip Carberry. He apologized for not taking me in to see his father.

'I'm afraid he's not good company at present. Financial worries are getting him down.'

'I quite understand. There's no need, anyway.'

He screwed up his face in anxious query. 'What happens next?'

'I talk to Jeremy and the other trustees. Then we either say no, or we indicate what offer we can make. Tell me: are the other members of the family in agreement with the idea of disposing of the Collection?'

He bit his lip. 'I think so. It's a bit difficult. Liz – that's Elizabeth, my sister – she's all for selling up. My brother James is not quite as keen. I undertook to sound Jeremy out after a rather heated family meeting. It all depends. The Collection is insured for three million right now, as Jeremy has probably told you.' He smiled shyly as I swore mentally at a Jeremy who has often omitted to impart such boring things as facts to me. 'I shouldn't tell you, but Liz said we should go for anything we can get over two million, whereas James says it's not worth selling for anything under five. I think it's only fair to let you know how things stand. I'm the pig in the middle, if you like. I'm just trying to see if we can take such steps quietly and logically before they're forced on us by circumstances. I know I can trust you and White's to be fair; I've checked and everyone says so.'

'Thank you.'

'I really don't want the world to know that we're considering selling. An auction with a lot of publicity wouldn't help us at all right now. That's why the personal contact with Jeremy is so important. I mean, in these circumstances, I feel I should put my cards on the table. There has to be trust. If, of course, you give it a thumbs-down, we shall have to go back to the drawing-board, so to speak.'

He peered at me anxiously, waiting for some sort of signal. Beside me, the presence of Sue emanated restricting waves upon any reply. I decided that cowardice and temporization were the only, however weak, courses to follow.

'Of course. It's clearly an interesting proposition, even though we have no precedent for buying it. A whole collection, I mean. Or of equestrian art. It isn't up to me alone, Philip, but I'll be in touch as soon as I can.'

'Thanks very much.'

He really seemed quite grateful. We shook hands, got in the car, and trundled back over the moat. I drove swiftly back down the road to a further village where there was a pub and went in, with Sue, to order a drink before we'd exchanged a word.

'Well,' she said, once a gin and tonic was in front of her on an alcove table. 'I admire the decisive manner.'

'There's no need to rub it in, Sue.'

'I'm sympathetic. I know it's hard to let someone down point-blank. But you can't possibly buy that assemblage of third-rate Boys' Own rubbish. Horses all over the place. Dozens of them. The father hasn't got any taste; no eye for a painting at all.'

'I rather liked the "Start at Newmarket",' I objected, mildly. 'And the horse fair, with gypsies.'

'Oh, yes, I suppose if you could pick them up cheap. That's quite a different thing. But all those boring horses; only Skeaping had any appeal to me, and his was a flash number.'

'It was a valuable lot of gear, though.'

'There were enough of Munnings's paintings to run up quite a bill, I agree, but at three million for insurance, my advice would be to buy a box of matches.'

'Sue, really! That's criminal.'

'Yes, it is. And you would know much more about what's criminal than me.' She took a strong swig of her gin and tonic, and looked expectantly at me. 'Why don't you admit it, Tim? The real reason why you're not really very much interested in that collection of horse nonsense – thank the Lord – is that your eye is right off the ball. You're still thinking about that blonde of Orpen's – Yvonne Aubicq – and hoping to find Ted Murphy's painting? Aren't you?'

'Of course not, Sue. How can you believe such a thing?'

She looked at me. I looked at her.

Then we both burst out laughing.

47

CHAPTER 6

Sergeant Will Cook eased himself slightly in his chair behind the table and looked appreciatively at the second glass of beer I placed in front of him.

'Cheers,' he said, with a faint smile. 'Here's to crime.'

I raised my own glass in respectful response. I found it unusual for a CID man to be a beer drinker; most of the CID men I've come across have gone for the hard stuff. Sergeant Will Cook, however, had a laudable, if rather outdated, taste for bottled Pale Ale.

We were in a pub on the Fulham Road not far from the late Ted Murphy's shop. It was an area I knew well; when Sue and I first started together I lived not more than four hundred yards from where we were sitting.

'I hope you don't think,' Cook said, after a suitable pull at his glass, 'that I'm circumventing DCI Roberts in any way, but I thought I would appreciate a quiet chat with you on the QT, so to speak.'

'Sure. I'm aware that you may have other questions to ask. I'm confident we won't tread on Nobby's toes or break any of his injunctions. Nothing like that.'

'No.' He smiled significantly. 'Well, to be fair, we've got the job of solving the crime. DCI Roberts is available to us in an advisory capacity, so to speak, but we have the task of getting the results.'

'Very true.'

'I mean, it won't be DCI Roberts who gets it in the neck if this thing isn't brought to book quick-sharp, so to speak.'

'No, it won't.' So to speak was obviously the in-phrase at Chelsea nick right now.

Cook let his smile disappear and spoke more questioningly. 'You said that Murphy used to bring paintings to you from time to time?'

'Yes, he did.'

'Did he ever have anyone with him? A colleague, a partner?'

'No, never.'

'A lady friend?' This time the question was put more directly.

'No.' It was true; I'd never met Ted in company with a woman. I assumed he had women friends, but he kept them away from his dealing life.

'Oh yes, I remember; you said you knew nothing about his private life.'

'Nope. I never met any of his girlfriends, if he had them.'

Cook smiled meaningfully. 'Oh, he had them. Between you and me, he seems to have had quite a varied private life, so to speak.'

'Really?'

'Oh, yes. Quite the dark horse, he was.'

'Good heavens.'

'Anyway – this card hinting at a painting he was going to bring up: did he send cards like that frequently? Pictures and so on?'

'Er, not usually, no. More often it was a phone call.'

'Any idea why he might have sent a card this time?'

'No, not really. He sent me a card of a Tissot once. A Tate Gallery thing. "HMS Calcutta". Turned out he expected to have a nice Thameside scene of Tissot's to sell. When it came it was, too. Nice, I mean. We bought it. We didn't always buy the things he presented, though.'

'Ah, so did he send a card when he was expecting something rather than actually having it? Then phone if he actually had it, then and there, so to speak?'

I considered. 'That's a possibility. I hadn't thought of it that way. You mean the card was a sort of advance warning?'

'Something like that. You say you haven't got the envelope it came in?'

'No, I'm sorry; I must have chucked it away at the office.'

'Pity. It would have been useful to know where he posted it.'

'Well, I'll have a look when I get back to the office. It may still be with the papers on my desk. I didn't think about it at the time, of course; I kept the card carefully to one side so the envelope may still be there. I naturally assumed he sent it from London.'

'Mmm.' Cook drew on his glass again. 'Not necessarily. He

bought it in London. I walked into a stationer's just down the road from here and saw some in stock. Identical, they were. The assistant remembered selling one to him four days ago.'

'Good heavens! Well done.'

Cook shrugged. 'It still doesn't help us much. It would be nice to know where he posted it, just to tie up loose ends. Please do have a look for us when you get back to your office. We need to know his last movements. You're sure you never saw him with a woman?'

'Positive.'

'Pity.' He drew on his glass again. 'You won't be able to help with that aspect, then.'

'Is it an important aspect?' I began to feel, from Cook's hints, that I had been slow on the uptake in some way.

'Rather. That's why I'm surprised you won't be able to help us. To connect one of his little snaps with someone.'

'Snaps?'

'Snaps, yes. Photographs. He had an album of them.'

'What, of girlfriends?'

'That's it. Quite a selection. Two books full. We found the albums in his desk. I don't know how far they go back – quite a while by the look of them – but he seems to have kept his memories with a photo pretty often.'

'Oh.' Cook was looking at me with what I can only call a meaning sort of look, as though the photos were pretty lurid or something. I didn't know what to say. Ted Murphy's private life had never been revealed to me, so I had no means of contributing and I started to feel a sense of intrusion. Ted was a quiet but humorous man, as I've said; an art school type, educated, sympathetic. I didn't want to hear nasty revelations.

Cook seemed to understand my reticence. 'Yes, it's a pity. I was going to ask you to look through them to see if there was anyone you recognized, but it'd be pointless if you couldn't connect them with Murphy.'

'No.'

'You knew, by the way, that his name wasn't really Murphy, did you?'

'Good grief, no. Of course I didn't.'

Cook smiled a satisfied sort of smile. 'No, he wasn't born Murphy. He was brought up by a family called Murphy here in

London and at some point when still a boy he took their name. His real surname was Pulham.'

'Pulham?'

'Yes, Pulham. From Dublin. His parents died when he was young and he was sent over here. The Murphys were distant relatives of some sort by marriage. They came from Dublin, too, but had settled in London.'

'I see.' I sat quite still. I suppose Murphy can become as English a name as Jack Robinson can become Irish, if enough time goes by. But Pulham; where did that come from?

'Yes. He was a bit of a mystery man, was chum Murphy.' Cook's voice had gone into a police-professional tone. 'I think there's a lot more to find out about him yet. It's my belief that we're looking for an angry husband.'

'Ah. A domestic affair once again?'

'I think so.' He grinned at me. 'Just as your friend DCI Roberts advised. But there might be a more complicated aspect. So if you can help us with that envelope and any other things that come to mind – I'd appreciate a call.'

'Of course.'

'I wouldn't like DCI Roberts to think I'm encouraging you, though.'

'Oh, no. Nothing like that.'

He grinned. 'From my reading of your file, domestic sorts of crimes aren't your cup of tea.'

'No.'

'Art's what really gets you going, isn't it?'

I smiled ruefully. 'I suppose so.'

He paused for a moment. 'Talking about art, you never told us what happened to that chap on the card – Grover-Williams – and the lady when the war broke out.'

'Oh. Well, it was rather tragic really. They joined the Resistance. With a French racing driver called Benoist. SOE ran them under the code-name Chestnut. They were very brave but the men got caught. Grover-Williams was tortured and sent to concentration camp. He never gave anything away. They kept him in solitary for a year at Sachsenhausen, then executed him.'

'Bastards.'

'She was arrested for a while, then let go, so she was lucky. She was heartbroken about Grover-Williams. They gave her a British widow's pension. After the war, she became a dog breeder in France and came over from time to time to be a judge at Cruft's. Scottish terriers; quite a few people remembered her, but she never talked about Orpen. Williams had become too dear to her. She died in the early 'seventies.'

I was going to say something more, but at that point, I stopped. The story of Yvonne Aubicq has always had particular poignancy for me and is deeply associated with the days when I lived in the Fulham Road. But I wasn't up to explaining about my side of it to anyone just then. Sergeant Cook and I parted company affably and I headed off back to the bank, keeping my thoughts to myself.

There was no point in telling Sergeant Will Cook that with dealers, art is always a domestic matter. I assumed that, being a Chelsea man, he'd know that already.

CHAPTER 7

Once I got back to the office, the rest of the day went very badly. Things went wrong as soon as I walked in.

'They have been waiting,' Penny said reprovingly, 'for about a quarter of an hour.'

I sat at my desk and frowned at her. '*They* haven't got an appointment.'

'I know. But they said it was urgent. I told them I was expecting you at two and that you hadn't got another appointment, so they said they'd come right away. They wanted to see Jeremy but he put them over to you. That was before the meeting was called for three.'

'Eh? Meeting? What meeting?'

'Jeremy has called a meeting of the available Art Fund trustees for three this afternoon. Sir Richard White is over from France.'

'Nobody ever tells me anything.'

'Well, you weren't in. You left here at noon.' Penny's fair features pinkened. 'And you did say you'd be back here at two.'

'I was delayed.'

'Evidently.'

'Bloody hell!'

Jeremy was going to stampede me. I could see it coming. I stared at Penny angrily.

'Who did you say these people were?'

'Mrs Dennison and Mr James Carberry. Mrs Elizabeth Dennison is his sister.'

'Jesus Christ! As though it weren't enough to have Jeremy pushing his luck, I've got the Crockinghams to deal with, have I?'

'They're waiting rather impatiently. Shall I show them in?'

'Is there any choice?'

I didn't even have time to look through the papers on my

desk, as I'd promised Will Cook. My eyes flicked round just once to make sure that the room looked reasonable before the visitors arrived; it is not large or anything like Jeremy's, but I have managed to extract one or two paintings from the Fund for my own enjoyment, and to add a couple of my own. The Orpen I told Nobby and Will Cook about hung to the side of me where I could see it, reminding me not only of Orpen and Yvonne Aubicq but also the late Morris Goldsworth, against whom I bid to secure it at auction. My own Bratby of George Melly, caked in colour, stared lop-eyed from opposite; the Fund's Nash of a cornfield glowed on the other wall.

There was just time to take it in before Penny ushered the visitors towards me, quick-sharp. They came straight through the door and stood in front of me expectantly, like a pair from a repertory theatre company who've practised their entrance and aren't going to let other stage events get in the way of their dogged performance.

The man reminded me of his father. He was nothing like his brother, Philip. A stocky frame and a face reddening from outdoor exposure or brewer's flush were set under a bush of unruly black hair. Blue puffy eyes stared at me with bloodshot arrogance. He wore a pinstripe suit which had bold stripes twice the width of mine, giving him the prominence of a chalked blackboard. The frontal area was nearly as full as his father's already; in a few years he'd be well into the blood pressure stakes.

The lady was quite different. She was tastefully dressed and slender, with a clear skin and brown hair. I put her at a couple of years older than me, but that diminished her attraction not a bit. She had hazel eyes which regarded me appraisingly and coolly without any of the brother's arrogance. She was much more like Philip, but she emanated a far greater confidence; in a family dominated by that father and, presumably, this brother in front of me, she had clearly learned to use her female status wisely. I wondered who her husband was as I noticed her eyes leave me to flick briefly round the walls, taking in the paintings.

'I must apologize,' I said, standing to shake hands with them, 'for the fact that you were kept waiting. I was delayed.'

'Not at all,' she said, before her brother could say anything. 'We came on the off chance and it's good of you to see us so quickly.'

She didn't say that with a customer as important to the bank as the Carberrys, she naturally expected to have instant attention, nor was it implied by her tone; her voice was pleasant, slightly high in pitch, and as she spoke she engaged my attention in a way I found suddenly flattering, as though I had become directly of interest to her.

'Please sit down,' I said. 'Can I offer you some coffee or anything?'

'No, thanks. Your secretary looked after us while we were waiting.' James Carberry's voice was deep and the diction slightly abrupt, as though he were in a hurry. 'But if you need some, go ahead.'

I sat down carefully as they did, without responding. I was not sure if his implication was that I had been overdoing lunch or was feeble in some way.

'What can I do for you?'

'The Collection,' he said, shortly. 'We came to talk to Jeremy White about it, but apparently he's tied up. You were the one who went to Crockingham, anyway?'

'Yes, I was.'

'Philip's a good chap, but not very decisive. He couldn't seem to say whether the news was that you were going ahead or not. You've seen everything to your satisfaction, haven't you?'

'Yes, I have.'

'Well, obviously I don't want to prejudice your internal processes, or whatever it is you do here at the bank, and so on, but we need to have an indication of what's happening pretty damn quick.'

'James.' Elizabeth Dennison's voice was both reproving and apologetic. She turned an appealing stare upon me. 'I'm sorry to put difficult questions to you, Mr Simpson, but we've just come from Lloyds. A meeting of names. It's been another disastrous year. Terrible. They announced the losses this morning. Two point nine billion. We – our family – are going to be horrendously hit. All over again. And probably more next year.'

'I'm very sorry to hear that.'

'We're suing the bastards, of course.' James Carberry's voice thickened with resentment. 'They needn't think we're going to let ourselves be fleeced by that gang of crooked insiders. Not without a fight.'

Financial disaster hits different people differently. Impotent rage, the reaction of the non-gambler who has gambled and lost for reasons he or she does not understand, is probably the most destructive form of stress there is. James Carberry's flushed face told its own story; he wanted to hit at something but there was no one about the place to hit. What chance there was of suing successfully seemed to me to be poor; if you join a game of poker and you lose, it's no good screaming at the dealer or binding about the way the cards were printed. His sister was composed; her head was held resolutely in a way that told of difficulties, but she had herself under control. Her eyes met mine appealingly.

'Mr Simpson, you said to Philip that you'd have to have a meeting of trustees before you could give us any decision. We'd like to know when that might be? The situation is critical for us, you see. We have to find funds very quickly. Even our properties – Crockingham Hall itself – could be under threat.'

I smiled inwardly. Jeremy's timing was often unerring.

'This afternoon. There is a meeting this afternoon at which the matter will be discussed.'

Her mouth opened slightly and then she smiled, not broadly but in a relieved way that went directly to me. 'That's quick. That's very quick. We're extremely grateful.'

'Of course it's quick. They've got to move fast if they want to get the Collection.' James had recovered something of his arrogance. 'Can't miss up a chance like this, eh, Simpson?'

'We like to think that our reactions are usually swift.'

'So when will we know how much?'

I bit my lip slightly, not liking his question or his direct stare. Elizabeth Dennison was looking at me more speculatively but, although not nearly as intense as her brother's, her regard seemed to penetrate my mind much more effectively. I was disconcerted.

'I can't say anything about the way things will go. Until the meeting is convened and the trustees have discussed the matter, I'm not free to make any guesses. It would be wrong to do so.'

'But you'll give us your offer pretty quick?' James Carberry was not to be put off.

'We have never bought a complete collection like this before. Nor have we invested in equestrian art. It was not our original intention, so it is a different decision to consider.'

Elizabeth Dennison's eyes, which I was watching, widened

fractionally and she leant slightly forward to look at me a little more closely.

'But that's your omission, obviously.' James Carberry was still on the aggressive. 'You've missed out there, if you don't mind my saying so. Time to make up for it now.'

'That's for the trustees to decide.' My voice was not quite as neutral as it should have been.

'But you're for it, aren't you, Simpson? Surely? The purchase, I mean? It's a damned good collection, isn't it?'

'I like the Munnings paintings very much.'

'Good. Well, that's settled, then. Can I use your phone?'

'Certainly.' Pleased to have any sort of diversion, I pushed the instrument across to him. Elizabeth Dennison was still look-ing at me, but when I gave her a direct look in exchange, her eyes flicked away, back to the paintings on the walls.

James Carberry dialled, waited, then spoke.

'Father? James. We're with Simpson now. The meeting is this afternoon. Of course. Will you? Right. 'Bye.'

He put the instrument down and stood up. 'Right. Good. We'll leave you to do the necessary. Liz? I think we should get along for now. We can hear about the meeting afterwards. Let 'em get on with it.'

She stood up carefully, looking at the Orpen of himself and Yvonne Aubicq in the studio, the languorous blonde nude stretched on the sofa, mirror-reflected. She moved closer to it, looking at the nude figure intently as though trying to recognize it.

'What a super painting,' she said, looking back to me. 'Who painted it?'

'Orpen. Sir William Orpen. That's a self-portrait; he liked using mirrors in his paintings. To great effect.'

She frowned slightly and turned to her brother. 'Didn't Father buy an Orpen, years ago?'

'Not unless it was a horse. Father only buys horse paintings. Or rather, *bought* horse paintings. No, I'm sure there was no Orpen. No horses, you see.'

She turned back to me. 'He was Irish, wasn't he?'

'Yes. Actually, the Orpens came originally from Norfolk. Anglo-Irish Protestant stock.'

'Ah.' A puzzled look came to her face. 'I could have sworn — but no, I don't remember. We mustn't take up your time.'

'You are very welcome to my time.'

If, I thought to myself, there were an Orpen in the Crockingham Collection, then I might be more enthusiastic about it. But Orpen and horses don't go together. I could, however, be enthusiastic about her. There was a lot to attract a man about her; a certain air, an unknown knowledge some women seem to exude.

She was still looking at me appraisingly, as though not seeing me for the first time; it was disconcerting.

'Will you please let me know as soon as a decision is made? I shan't be going to Crockingham with James.'

'Of course.'

'My telephone number is –'

She gave me a number to take down. I noted it on my pad.

'It's in the Cambridge area,' she said. 'Fen Ditton. I have a cottage up there.'

'Fine.'

She didn't say 'we' have a cottage up there. Suddenly I got the feeling that there wasn't a Mr Dennison any more.

'I expect I'll hear up at Crockingham when you phone my father,' James said. 'I hope the figure will be up to the reputation of White's Bank.'

I held out my hand. 'Please excuse me; I must go to the meeting now.'

He paused, disconcerted by my lack of reaction, shook my hand briefly and went to the door.

She held my hand rather longer.

'Whatever transpires,' she said. 'I would love to hear more about the Art Fund, anyway.'

'It'll be my pleasure.'

They went out, Penny fluttering round to show them the way.

Leaving me wondering how the hell I was going to refuse to buy the Crockingham Collection after a charming invitation like that.

CHAPTER 8

They were sitting round the mahogany table in Jeremy's office when I got there. Jeremy had taken the chair. Geoffrey sat opposite my place, next to Sir Richard White.

'Hello, Tim.' Sir Richard's voice was cordial.

'Hello, Richard.'

I shook hands with him before I sat down. He looked as fit as ever for a man in his seventies. His light suit and crisp shirt were cut excellently to his slim figure. Sir Richard White lives mostly in France, dividing his time between the Dordogne, where he has both an elegant, ancient stone property and a large acreage of fruit and nut trees, and Paris where the Maucourt Frères Bank, with whom we are associated and of which he is a director, occupies his time. Every now and then he comes back to base in London. Sometimes unexpectedly.

Like now.

'I hear you've had visitors,' he said, his eyes twinkling slightly.

'You're very well informed.'

'I had a call from Sir Andrew Carberry. Two minutes ago.'

'Oh, dear.'

He smiled. Jeremy cleared his throat. Geoffrey gave me a cautious stare. So James Carberry had signalled his father and his father had not wasted a minute. Straight on the blower to Sir Richard.

'His son was smart off the mark,' I said.

'Indeed he was.'

'Tell me – is there a Mr Dennison? The sister's husband, I mean?'

Sir Richard's eye twinkled even more. 'Not for some time. Mr Dennison got the boot a while ago. Mrs Dennison is a divorcée.'

'Ah.'

'An attractive lady.'

'She is, indeed.'

'Very independent.'

'Oh?'

Sir Richard's twinkle died a little. 'A modern lady, I think one might say.'

'Ah.'

I didn't get a chance to draw Sir Richard out to explain what he meant by modern, or even independent, in this context because there then intruded some impatient and much louder throat-clearing noises which mean, usually, that Jeremy wants the floor to himself. We all respectfully fell silent.

'I think we can call a start to the meeting.' Jeremy's tone was brisk. 'We haven't a full board of trustees, of course, but sufficient for a quorum and, effectively, the executive members are all present. I've called the meeting a bit suddenly, for which I apologize, but due to events this morning – the disaster at Lloyds we all knew about is now official – there is pressure for a quick decision. I refer, of course, to the Crockingham Collection.'

He paused to peer at me from under his blond locks. I sat motionless, thinking a bit about Elizabeth Dennison and looking at the file I'd brought with me.

'At my behest,' Jeremy went on, slightly hurried, perhaps due to my lack of reaction, 'Tim has been to look at the Collection to make a preliminary assessment. I think before we go any further we should hear his report and recommendations.'

'I agree.' Sir Richard nodded approvingly. 'Let us by all means hear Tim's report.'

I gave him a quick glance before starting but his face was expressionless. I get on well with Sir Richard nowadays, having been somewhat at odds in the past, when Jeremy and I belonged to a faction that was too pushy for Sir Richard and the Old Guard at the bank. Their teeth had been drawn by Jeremy's clever politicking and Sir Richard somewhat duffed-up, but he had forgiven us. That was all history now. Hatchets had been buried, fences mended, bygones bygoned and similar emollient clichés enacted. In fact, I now quite frequently work for Sir Richard; when his cultured nose smells a rat his first reaction is to whistle up his terrier in my usually reluctant form. But for some reason, his presence and demeanour today were disturbing. There was too set an expression about him; it occurred to me that Jeremy had shipped him over specially for this get-together in case Geoffrey took my side.

'I have seen the Collection.' I tapped the file in front of me. 'It consists of mostly British paintings of the early twentieth century – but there are one or two nineteenth-century items – including sculptures. All of an equestrian nature. The principal artist in the collection is Munnings, who has, of course, a somewhat local interest. There is also a small Stubbs, or at least a painting attributed to Stubbs, because I've not checked the provenance, which is eighteenth-century. I have the catalogue of the Collection here and have seen most of the items depicted or described myself.'

'Good. Excellent. So what do you think?' Jeremy was still brisk.

'We have never bought a complete collection before. Nor have we bought equestrian art before. Not because there is anything written into the Fund's rules about it, but because either the opportunity has not arisen, or because it has not been our liking or policy. We have tended to buy paintings by artists whose work was original and innovative rather than traditional.'

'Yes, we know that. But there has to be a first time for everything.' Jeremy sounded reasonable, like a man who prepares for resistance but is determined to be calm.

'I know. But I do not recommend that we buy the Collection. There are a lot of boring paintings in it. The hunting scenes are not too bad and there are general, sort of country, things which are good, but the horse portraits are pretty tedious when seen *en masse*. I recommend that we tell the Carberrys that if they must sell it – regrettably – they put the Collection into auction at Christerby's where its fair market value will be realized. Then we can buy a couple of the Munnings fair and square, leaving the rest.'

Stunned silence for a moment. Or rather not stunned; suddenly, looking at their set faces, I knew they were expecting this, or at least anticipating it. Just silence for a moment. Geoffrey looked at the table top. Jeremy's face creased in disapproval. Then Sir Richard spoke, gravely, quietly, without emotion.

'I am afraid,' he said, 'that from the Carberrys' point of view your recommendation has grievous disadvantages, Tim. One, to prepare the Collection for auction will take time. They haven't got much time. Two, it will mean the break-up of the Collection.

Three, the commission taken at auction will effectively deduct fifteen to twenty per cent of the value realized at a time when the market is not strong. Four, it will mean that the gallery in which the Collection is housed will end its existence, its local presence. And five, it would assist the Carberrys best if this transaction remained confidential until an announcement of a *fait accompli* can be made, thus better reassuring their creditors than the lottery of a future auction would do.'

I nodded understandingly. 'I entirely agree. I would rather the Carberrys did not have to sell the Collection. I sympathize, to a certain extent, with their predicament and their need to maintain confidence. But I do not want the Fund to buy this collection in one job lot. I do not think that that is in the Fund's best interests.'

Sir Richard did not appear to hear me. 'There are, also, some other factors to take into account.'

'Oh?'

Jeremy leant forward. 'The Carberrys are major clients of ours. We have acted for them over many years. Richard, in particular, has acted for Sir Andrew in a role of adviser. In earlier days we had a lot of takeover business from Sir Andrew.'

'Before or after he was an MP?'

'Both.'

'And during?'

'Tim, there is no need for unpleasant implications. We have an obligation to help an important client who is heavily invested through us.'

'I'm aware of that. Far be it from me to wish to upset the bank's relationships. But I have my Art Fund hat on right now.'

'As quite rightly you should.' Jeremy managed an approving tone. 'Disregarding, however, whether the paintings are boring or not, what value do you put on the Collection? A reasonable estimate in today's conditions?'

'In today's market they'd be lucky, at auction, to be left with more than one and a half million for it after commission and expenses. If I wanted to buy it, which I don't, that's what I'd pay for it.'

'Nonsense!' Jeremy's eyes bulged. 'It's insured for three million.'

'So what?'

Geoffrey, I noticed, had sat up at this.

'Tim, it was valued for insurance only –'

'Three years ago. Things were booming then.'

'It can't have gone down all that much! Not equestrian art!'

'Have you looked at the horse racing world lately?'

Sir Richard held up his hand. 'Gentlemen, gentlemen. Let us not get away from the realities. We have been offered a substantial and valid collection of paintings in a specialist field which has a value. Tim says one thing and Jeremy says another. That is not the point right now. The decision we have to take is whether – within a certain figure, I agree, depending on the Fund's resources – we should buy it or not. After that decision we have to agree a price with the owner.'

'Quite right,' said Jeremy.

'The two are inseparable, Richard.' I was going to lose this; I could feel it coming. This meeting was rigged.

'Tim, Tim. Please wait. Let me finish. If the owner will not agree a figure then I accept that we can't buy the Collection. I think it will be much easier than you imagine, though. The owner is in dire straits right now but it would be wrong of the bank to take advantage of that. Besides, in absolute extremity the owner could do as you suggest and go to auction. The thing here is that Sir Andrew Carberry doesn't want to do that for the reasons I've outlined, and because he wants to keep the Collection together. It's psychologically important to him. He also wants to keep the Collection at Crockingham for a reasonable period in the future. The local interest is a sort of obligation; people in the area should be able to see their own art, so to speak. He phoned me to suggest that if we bought the whole Collection it could be kept where it is – subject to the usual insurance safeguards – even though it would, of course, become an asset of the Fund's. After all, it has to be stored somewhere.'

'Cunning beggar. Wants to eat his cake and have it.'

'He is willing to consider any reasonable offer – he would prefer the insurance value but agrees that things are not very good just now – providing we agreed to leave the Collection where it is for a specified period. Five years is what he suggests. He also points out that, taking the longer term view, the Collection is bound to recover in value and the Fund will benefit from this.'

'Quite right.' Jeremy nodded emphatically.

I felt myself going hot. 'We are not the National Art

Collections Fund. It is not our business to preserve individual collections. We have a duty to our investors.'

'And this will fulfil it.' Jeremy was getting irritable with me. 'The value of the Collection is bound to rise. But I fully take Tim's point that the value may have altered in current circumstances. As I understand it, James Carberry won't agree, but other members of the family would be willing to accept two million. I think that Sir Andrew is being very reasonable about the whole thing. Keeping the Collection where it is would have good PR vibes for the Fund, too. Show us as sensitive investors. I think we should offer them two million. That would be a fair compromise.'

'Thirty per cent over the odds?'

He almost ground his teeth. 'There are other factors, Tim! The Carberrys have large amounts invested with us! Much more than two million. Their portfolio may have to be realized in large sums to meet their Lloyds obligations.'

'So for the bank's benefit you want to use the Fund's spare cash to prop up the Carberrys' property, shares and other mistakes?'

'Tim, *really*! I'll ask you to withdraw that!'

'Sorry. I withdraw it. Unreservedly.'

'Thank you.'

He managed to look mollified. Geoffrey was looking decidedly unhappy. Sir Richard leant forward. 'Come on, Tim, you'd buy a collection of Picassos at the right price, wouldn't you, even if you hated Picasso's work?'

'I suppose I would. At the right price. Knowing that Picasso is not only an original, but always a saleable, commodity.'

'So is equestrian art.'

'I don't think so. Not if you don't own the horse, don't remember it, and the painting is not very exciting.'

'But you like the Munnings?'

'Yes, I do.'

'Well, that's only a personal preference, isn't it? Other people might like the Dupont, or the Skeaping. Down in the Camargue where Skeaping lived, the horsemen thought Skeaping was way better than Picasso.'

I smiled. 'I remember that. But I just don't think we should swallow this whole lot in one gulp.'

He sat back and shook his head. 'Well, I have to agree with

Jeremy. We have to take a broader view. A bank view. The fund must invest rather than conserve cash. Here is an opportunity. I think the time has come to vote. Jeremy?'

'Certainly, Richard. Geoffrey?'

So that was when they out-voted me.

Three to one.

I could see that Geoffrey didn't like it; Geoffrey is an accountant and he hates buying above the market price. He trusts my judgement in things like that. But Geoffrey had doubtless been persuaded to take the 'broader view', meaning the insider-bank's view, not the way we would normally have bought. The whole broad set of figures said too much for him. So it was my day to lose.

I managed to get a stay of execution for the normal assessment to be made by an expert, someone from Christerby's, because all our purchases are vetted by an expert for authenticity. Sir Richard undertook to give Sir Andrew the glad tidings down at Crockingham. He hesitated for a moment as the meeting broke up, looked as though he was going to say something to me, looked at Jeremy, and didn't.

I went back to my office to sit down and glare at my desk. Jeremy had got his way. I was angry but it wasn't something to resign over; I'd defeated Jeremy on purchases I wanted in the past. Both of us could take it as well as hand it out. Without getting into a huff.

Well, not too much of a huff.

But something of a huff.

Rather a bloody huff, in fact.

After a short while, Penny came in rather timidly and asked me if I'd like some tea. I said, yes, without using much charm. She brought it in, hung about for a moment, then said, 'Well, at least Daddy will be pleased.'

'What a consolation.' I couldn't help sounding sour. 'Why?'

'He likes horse paintings. Especially Munnings.'

'Well, he would, wouldn't he?'

'I mean, he'll probably invest in the Art Fund now. He wouldn't have before.'

'We have opened up a whole new tranche of investors.' I could hear Jeremy saying that, not myself.

She ignored my sarcastic tone. 'He didn't know that Munnings was one-eyed. I must say, I showed off a bit when he took me out to lunch yesterday. He was quite surprised; I think he thinks you may be educating me.'

'A grave responsibility,' I snarled, eyeing her wide hips thoughtfully.

She blushed pink. 'Well, I expect with all those Munnings paintings coming in, you'll become even more of an expert on him, too, won't you?'

She was trying to butter me up, poor girl, but I wasn't in the mood.

'Expert? I'll have to learn a hell of a lot more about him before I can claim to be an expert.'

'Oh? Haven't you got a lot of information about him and things, like you have for all the others? All those reference books and so on?'

I stared at her thoughtfully again. At her face this time, gazing at me in innocent query. She was quite right; I ought to mug up a bit on Munnings before we took in the whole of the Crockingham Collection.

I needed to get away from the bank for a bit, too. Right now, if possible.

'No, I haven't got much by way of literature about him,' I replied, getting up and swallowing her tea quickly. 'But thanks very much for reminding me, Penny. I know a man who has.'

CHAPTER 9

Mr Goodston, sitting behind the heaped desk of his second-hand bookshop in Praed Street, looked even more like a caricature of Mr Toad of Toad Hall than the last time I visited him. His half-moon glasses, strung precariously across his face, flashed as he looked up from his sporting papers to take in my entrance. His pop eyes bulged in recognition.

'Mr Simpson! This is a surprise! And, I need hardly add, a pleasure!'

His seat creaked cordially. His bulky form shifted, but did not rise, in a movement intended to convey respect without causing effort. A scatter of papers wafted to the floor. Mr Goodston is a cautious, fat man of great expertise who surrounds himself with ranks of dingy, subfusc literary bindings and the accumulated debris of years of betting on horses. Mr Goodston is not just an antiquarian book connoisseur in what he jovially calls sporting, military and thespian specialities. He is also a punter. A dedicated punter. His weakness consumes his literary profits. If his shop is closed, you know that Mr Goodston is lining the pockets of the nearest bookmaker or, more rarely, attending one of the classic events in order to do the same thing. Bookmakers, to my knowledge, do not accept telephone bets from Mr Goodston. They demand cash up front. On the other hand, for Mr Goodston, the invention of television has come as a huge boon; he can watch most races without having to move from his chair. From this vigil he can decide whether it is worthwhile bestirring himself to the nearest betting shop in order to lose more money, or not.

In one corner of the shop, a handsome set with a large screen stood lifeless; it was shop closing time but Kempton Park, Haydock and the rest must have been temporarily inactive.

'Good afternoon, Mr Goodston. The pleasure is mine.'

I have used the services of Mr Goodston on·many occasions.

He positively spoils me when I go to see him. I suspect that the reason for this is not so much that he values my purchases, as that most of his clientele is elderly; indeed more elderly than Mr Goodston himself, and he is far from young. They are interested in periods and events which few now recall. The younger generation are not prominent among them. In carrying out background research for the Art Fund, I have often needed to acquire biographical details from the nineteenth and early twentieth century quite extensively. Mr Goodston has been a rich source. The world of art, sport, the theatre and music considerably overlapped with that of politicians, soldiers and sailors years ago, when many of the artists in whom I have invested for the Fund were in full spate. Mr Goodston enjoys tracing these abutments and interrelationships with me; there is, additionally, nothing like a whiff of scandal to get him going.

'My dear boy! How well you look! To what do I owe the pleasure? The stage again? Miss Lily Langtry?' He put a finger to his nose. 'Or yet less celebrated scandals? An artist's model, perhaps? Kittie Newton? Or another frisson from Edwardian society?'

'Not this time, Mr Goodston.' I closed the door and came across to his desk to view the lists of runners marked with the blue-pencilled hieroglyphics which denote Mr Goodston's personal system. 'I am come to the oracle. A subject which I hope – indeed I know – will be close to your heart.'

His eyebrows went up. Mr Goodston knows that I am not a gambler, nor, in normal circumstances, at all interested in horse racing.

'Oracle? You flatter me, my dear sir. You flatter me. Mount Olympus is, I fear, far from this shore. No Greek deities flit across my humble shelves.'

He gestured sadly. The interior was, to be sure, looking gloomier than ever. None of the merchandising tricks, the bins of coloured paperbacks and brightly-crayoned cards which mark the modern book dealer, were to be seen. Fusty rows of volumes darkened the premises in tenebrous gravity. Stacks of encyclopedias, or perhaps the proceedings of learned societies, and bound blocks of regimental records rose in teetering columns from the squalid carpet. Things did not look active. Mr Goodston's commerce was not a brisk one. Only in the vicinity of his desk, where racing papers and tattered bloodstock magazines mingled in confused abandon, was there any indication of enthusiasm. Outside, the occasional red bus thundered past the dusty window, but no pedestrian stopped to peer in at the literature set behind the glass on a wide shelf in uninviting confusion.

Nothing had changed.

'Sir Alfred Munnings,' I said, watching him closely. 'Autobiography. The three volumes of.'

His face lit up. He snapped his racing formbook shut. A tremor shook his bulky frame.

'Munnings? Munnings? My very dear sir! For the Fund? White's Art Fund?'

'Ssh.' I placed a finger to my lips. 'This is absolutely Top Secret. I am here incognito, Mr Goodston. Nothing, absolutely, nothing, not even a breath, is to be breathed –'

He quivered in interruption. 'My dear Mr Simpson! You insult me! You know full well that all transactions here, even rumours of transactions, are utterly confidential! Utterly!'

'I am sorry, Mr Goodston. I apologize. Unreservedly. Of course they are. I know they are. It is just that, in this case, there is a particularly delicate aspect to the little investigation I am making. The, er, the vendor wants total confidentiality.'

He put a finger to his nose again. 'I understand. I understand completely. Say no more, my dear sir. Mum's the word. After all, it would be most embarrassing, I am sure, if it were to get out that, that White's Art Fund, was going to – to – well – how can I put it –?'

'What?'

'Buy the Crockingham Collection?'

I managed to avoid a heart attack, but it was a near thing. The shop reeled around me. Mr Goodston looked up with a mixture of plump concern and impish delight which put me in mind of a film of Winston Churchill baiting a parliamentary opponent.

I sat down on a very dirty spare chair in order to get my breath back.

'Is it as obvious as that?'

He beamed genially. I had made his evening. 'Merely a question of quick deduction, my dear Watson. The racing world is an incestuous one, riven by rumour. The Carberrys, once good patrons of the Turf, are in dire financial straits. Lloyds losses, poor earnings, slow horses, the odd Stock Exchange revenge from antagonists goaded by Sir Andrew's past misdemeanours. Rumours of the possible sale of their stable have been rife for weeks. In the inner racing world their painting collection is well known. It contains many of Munnings's works. *Ergo*, what more logical than to sell it? *Ergo*, who possible as a buyer? Through my very door comes the luminary, the very star of White's Art Fund to inquire about Munnings's memoirs in the context of making a discreet investment from an even discreeter client.' He smiled broadly. 'Here in Praed Street the world comes to us, my dear boy. Sooner or later the world comes to us.'

'I sit chastened, Mr Goodston. I beg your discretion all the same.'

'You have it! Of course you have it!' He heaved his bulk up from his chair and made a stately step away from the desk. 'Sir Alfred Munnings. President of the Royal Academy from 1944 to 1949. He could write, actually. *An Artist's Life*. Published, if I am not mistaken, in 1950. Museum Press. Illustrated by the author's own sketches.' He readjusted his glasses as he moved towards his shelves. '*The Second Burst* subsequently, published in 1952. Then *The Finish*, also 1952. I have all three volumes here, of course. Fine, in original dust wrappers. Ninety pounds, but to you, eighty.' He turned to raise his eyebrows at me dubiously. 'There is also an abbreviated version, a compendium published by Reader's Union in 1955; it is one volume and cuts out a good deal, but at a modest tenner if –'

'The full three volumes, please, Mr Goodston.'

He nodded approvingly. 'Of course, of course. The right decision, if I may say so. I also have a copy of Jean Goodman's biography, Collins 1988, entitled *What A Go!*, at fifteen pounds, if you –'

'That too, Mr Goodston.'

'Excellent.' He smiled happily. 'You have never been a man to cut corners, if you'll forgive my saying so. Young men today are usually so impatient. It warms my heart to find a younger bibliophile sticking to the old traditions. Thorough research always pays, my dear boy; I do not have to tell you that. Not you, of all people.'

He put the volumes down on the desk in front of him. The autobiography's three volumes were each wrapped in a buff dust jacket with a maroon border enclosing the title and charcoal sketches of the author painting at an easel, floating

celestially with horses, arguing with two companions at a con-
vulsed table surrounded by discarded bottles and broken wine-
glasses. The biography's jacket had an illustration of a painting
not unlike that at Crockingham. Mr Goodston smiled at me
blandly. It was as though he had anticipated my visit. Perhaps
he had. I stared at him thoughtfully.

'Munnings, Mr Goodston; can you tell me about him?'

'Tell you? Tell you what?'

'What do you think about him?'

'Good gracious, my dear young sir, do you want the full three-
day lecture course or merely my ten thousand word précis?'

'As briefly as you can, Mr Goodston.'

He sat back heavily in his chair, which creaked less cordially
under its responsibility. He stared loftily at the stained yellow
ceiling of his premises for a moment, as though composing himself, then spoke ruminatively.

'Munnings, eh? He could paint horses all right. With only
one eye. Superb. Better than the rest with two. He liked gypsies,
but had none of Augustus John's pretentious nonsense about
them; they understood Munnings well. And liked him. He
swore horribly, drank too much, played and worked like a fiend.
He made many enemies. He wrote well, rode to hounds,
composed ballads, poetry and coarse doggerel, was a friend of
Masefield's. He was disgracefully rude, often excessive, very
much the nineteenth-century English countryman. He would
fight over a twopenny extra on the bill. Swore at Laura Knight
for costing him a shilling for a bath. Spent money like water on
champagne. He was outstandingly generous.'

'Women?'

'His marriages were, I believe, disastrous. Both women looked
good on a horse. His first wife committed suicide. The second
and he were devoted in their way, but it was an odd way. She
was an excellent horsewoman. No children. Separate bedrooms.
Arguments. She'd married before, not well. He went off one
Christmas to France and left her on her own, with little dogs.
She always carried one of 'em with her, in her muff. A peke.
Black Knight, he was called. Went to the Lord Mayor's banquet
with it in her muff, so the Lord Mayor made it an Honorary
Freeman of the City of London. Did a book about it. She used
to run his finances. Gave him a fiver a day to spend, and that
was it. They had filthy rows in public.'

71

'Mistresses?'

Mr Goodston shook his head. 'I think he only loved painting, country things, drink, horses, bawdy nights, swearing, acting the big man at gentlemen's clubs. Laura Knight was fond of him, though. A lot of women would have found him dreadful but some said he had great charm. Modern feminism would try to stamp him out. He had a strong sense of humour. He was like a bull in a china shop. He worked very hard. He knew he wasn't a great artist but he tried his best. Larger than life. When he started painting, there were no motor cars. It was all horses, and men who looked after horses. He hated modern England. Hated it. Hated modern painting. Had some nasty opinions. Shouted them out loud. Was deeply hated in return.'

'He sounds a bit like a stallion without any mare to – to – calm his –'

'You put it well, my dear boy.' Mr Goodston brought his gaze down from the ceiling to stare at me. 'The unrequited male. That's a good image. Very good. He behaved like a bull without a herd. Booze had a lot to do with it though.'

'Poor chap.'

'He wouldn't have thanked you for sympathy! Not at all! Very aggressive, he was.'

'You seem to have made quite a study of him. You have strong feelings about him, Mr Goodston. I can tell.'

He smiled ruefully. 'The Turf, my dear young sir, the Turf. Inevitably. You know my passions. Actually –' he hesitated.

'What?'

'I had quite an experience once. I met him.'

'Really? When?'

Mr Goodston allowed a sad expression to cross his face. 'The late 'fifties, it must have been. I was very young, of course.'

'Of course.'

He ignored my assurance as an irreverence. 'I had a copy of *The Anatomy of the Horse* by Stubbs. Original 1766. In superb nick with all the plates engraved by Stubbs himself. A fantastic, valuable work. All equestrian artists use it. The good ones, anyway. I deliberately bumped into Munnings at Newmarket – got a jockey pal to introduce me – and asked if he was interested. He had a copy, of course, but this one of mine was exceptional. He told me to bring it to his house. Castle House, Dedham.' Another misty, reminiscent look crossed Mr Goodston's face. 'I made a special journey. It was the most important thing I had in stock at the time. Do you know what he did? I walked up the drive, rang the front doorbell and he opened up. Then he glared at me and told me to go to the back door. Swore at me. "Bloody tradesman," he said. "The bloody back door's for the likes of you. Tradesman's entrance." '

'Did he now?' I said, softly.

'He did. I was mortified. The sale of that book was very important to me, but I wasn't standing for that. You may find it surprising, but I was a hot-headed lad, Mr Simpson. Things were different then. "Tradesman, eh?" I shouted back at him. "That's rich, coming from a dusty miller's son. A poster-printer's boy giving himself airs. Chocolate biscuits to you! To hell with you! Gentleman dauber now, are you? Too grand, eh? I thought you were a professional. If you weren't so old I'd punch you one." And I stamped off down the drive, carrying my precious Stubbs with me.'

'Bully for you!' I must admit I was surprised; the Mr Goodston I knew was nothing like this.

'Do you know what he did?'

'What?'

Mr Goodston chuckled. 'He ran after me. Caught me by the arm. Made me come inside. He had great charm when he wanted. Then he disappeared and came back with two huge glasses of cask sherry. Tumbler size, they were. Strong as brandy, it was. Nothing like the Celebration Cream you and I occasionally enjoy. Firewater. Made me cough. He laughed delightedly at me. "You've got spirit, young shaver," he said. "Remind me of myself when I was your age. When I did chocolate biscuit and bicycle advertisements. Speak your mind like a good 'un. You'll get on, you will. Come on, drink up and show me your Stubbs." '

'Did he buy it?'

'No, he didn't. His was nearly as good. But he gave me an introduction to someone who did buy it. And a lot more. And he recommended me to all sorts of people. Good buyers, all of them. He was odd like that. I think the aggressive exterior hid something very soft, you know. He was delighted to get a reaction, that was it. Like gypsies who fight over a horse deal then go off to get drunk together. The country boy from nowhere who'd become President of the Royal Academy and was commissioned to paint royalty. His name's mud at the RA now, of course. A lot of his behaviour was a shell. He was very generous to many people who needed it. But he swore at Rothenstein for promoting Jewish artists because he was a Jew. Anti-Semitic. Not very nice at all.'

'Good grief.'

'Rothenstein got his own back by never hanging Munnings's Chantrey painting up in the Tate. Even though it was of royalty.'

'Oh dear.'

Mr Goodston's eyes held mine compellingly for a moment. 'Forgive me: you've never bought equestrian art or a complete collection before, have you?'

'No, we haven't.'

'Do you want to?'

'Not really.'

Mr Goodston made a gesture of query. 'Then, forgive me, I do not want to lose the sale of books, naturally, but why?'

'Pressure, Mr Goodston. Out of my hands, shall we say. Other factors to consider.'

He put his finger to his nose. 'Say no more, my dear young sir, say no more. I shall keep the silence of the grave.'

I stood up, paid him for the books, took them under my arm.

The silence of the grave. I wondered how Ted Murphy was finding it.

As though reading my thoughts, Mr Goodston looked up from his invoicing. 'I was sorry to hear about the death of Murphy,' he said. 'He wasn't a book man, of course, but our paths occasionally crossed, at auction. He was also a sometime customer for art books, like you. I believe you knew him quite well.'

'Yes, I did; professionally; no more.'

'Tragic,' he murmured.

'They haven't charged anyone yet.'

'*Cherchez la femme*.' It was just a murmur.

'I beg your pardon?'

'Nothing, nothing. He was a racegoer, lately. I saw him – but no, it's not relevant.'

'A racegoer? Where?'

'Newmarket.' Mr Goodston then frowned to himself. I waited, but no more came from him.

I tried to draw him. 'He sent me a note the day before his

death, Mr Goodston. To the bank. I was going to meet him. About a painting, possibly an Orpen. It was a hell of a shock.'

'Really?' He put his head back to quote. '"O that a man might know the end of this day's business, ere it come."'

'Er, quite. Shakespeare?'

'Indeed. *Julius Caesar.*'

'Ah. It was an odd thing. He signed himself Sergeant Murphy. I couldn't make it out. I mean, he wasn't in the army or anything. Or the police. Ever.'

Mr Goodston smiled sadly. 'Nor a National winner, either, one presumes.'

'Sorry?'

'A National winner.' He cocked his head curiously at my incomprehension. 'The winner of the Grand National – 1923 – was a horse called Sergeant Murphy. Surely you recall that? The animal was painted by Sir William Orpen just to show what he could do. Orpen's one of your favourites, isn't he? He put it into the Academy. At the time, people said his horse was much better than Munnings's that year.'

I missed the last few words; his voice seemed to have gone far away and his image went off as my sight lost its focus.

Sergeant Murphy was a horse.

A bloody horse, not a human being.

What the hell did Ted mean?

Blinking to focus again, I found that Mr Goodston was staring at me with high concern.

'My dear boy, what on earth ails you?' He struggled to his feet in consternation. 'You look as though ghosts have got at you!'

CHAPTER 10

I said that the rest of the day went badly; it didn't stop when I got home.

Sue was furious.

'I'm not sure you shouldn't have resigned,' she spluttered. 'Really! I think Jeremy goes beyond the pale sometimes. Far too often, in fact. And Sir Richard wasn't exactly an ally, was he?'

My mind was still distracted by Mr Goodston. It's amazing how often such visits have that effect.

'Times are tough, Sue. People have a lot of pressure to take.'

'Including you! You really should have thrown the damned business out! It's a disgraceful affair.'

'It's not very pleasant, no.'

So Sergeant Murphy was a horse. What in hell had Ted been driving at?

'You just had to buckle under.' She sniffed. 'Geoffrey's a broken reed, as well.'

'Sue, Geoffrey has his pressures to take too – what do you mean, as well?'

'When I think of that load of rubbish you're going to take under your wing, I could – I could –'

'I quite like the Munnings.'

An Orpen of a horse? Or Yvonne Aubicq? Or both?

'Munnings! Munnings! That barbarian! Philistine! Foul-mouthed clown! Typical Academy throwback!' She gestured at the books I'd bought from Mr Goodston. 'Art for ignorant horse fanciers. Waste of money. Waste of time. Waste of the Fund.'

I was starting to feel nettled. Sue's lot at the Tate really are as arrogant as Munnings himself when it comes to bigoted opinions.

'The Tate's bought more than a few howlers in its time, Sue.'

'That's got nothing to do with it. We're not proud of them.

The Chantrey Bequest has occasionally bought some terrible stuff, I agree, but not for nasty, greedy, sycophantic, boot-licking commercial reasons.'

'Just bad taste? Or merely personal prejudice?'

She harrumphed. 'I'm amazed at you. I don't know how you're going to live with that collection of wall-eyed, spavined, knock-kneed —'

'Pick of the bloodstock industry?'

'Horses! I mean, *horses*. Dull ones, too.'

'Not all of them.'

The original Sergeant Murphy painting would be traceable; I didn't think it would be that one. I really needed to do some research.

'And as for keeping it up there in that timbered mausoleum: my God, but White's Bank are a weak lot. They should have told Carberry to stuff that. No chance.'

'Local interest, Sue. It's got to be stored somewhere, anyway. There is an argument in its favour.'

'Rubbish! That crook Carberry will strut and preen himself, giving it about that he's eating his cake and having it. He'll make you look fools. You'll see.'

'He hasn't accepted the offer yet, Sue.'

'He will. Oh, he will. He's no fool. He's done so many sharp deals in the past it doesn't bear thinking about. Now he's put one over you. Too high a price *and* he keeps the Collection. Utter weakness. You should have put your foot down.'

It was time to deal with Sue; I shut my mind to Sergeant Murphy and addressed her shortly.

'I voted against. That's democracy. I've won my rounds in the past and now I've lost one. It's no more than that, and it's no good crying over spilt milk.'

'Rubbish! The Whites are doing just what they please with the Art Fund's money. There might as well be no trustees.'

'That,' I said, practically through clenched teeth, 'is simply not true.'

'Pah!' she said. Or it might have been faugh. Either way, it didn't help. She disappeared into the kitchenette and made pan-rattling noises, as though she was going to cook something, but I knew she wasn't. I threw myself, rather than sat, irritably into the armchair which has the telephone beside it. More

77

rattling noises came from Sue, together with another exclamation of anger.

I got out my pad, looked at it, thought for a moment, then
dialled the Cambridge number.

'Hello?'

Elizabeth Dennison's voice had rather a musical tone down
the telephone line.

'Mrs Dennison? This is Tim Simpson. I promised to give you
a ring.'

'Oh, how kind! What news?' It was a soft voice, a welcoming
voice, bringing her rather knowing persona instantly to mind.

'Good, from your point of view. The Fund have voted to offer
you two million for the Collection. And offered to leave it in
place at Crockingham.'

There was silence for a moment. Then her voice came back,
thoughtfully. 'That's very good news for the family.'

'Indeed.'

'Although I shall be sad that the Collection will pass out of
our hands.'

'I suppose so.'

Her tone changed to curiosity. 'Would I be wrong in thinking
you were not really in favour?'

'Er, I had my reservations, yes.'

'I thought so. I quite understand. Tim' – the tone softened to
intimacy – 'may I call you Tim?'

'Of course.'

'I'm Liz to my friends. Tim, there's something I think you
ought to know. Something I can't talk about on the phone.'

Her voice had gone quiet, as though she were afraid of being
overheard.

'Really?'

'Yes. Could we meet?'

'Of course.' It would have been impossible for any man to
say no to that; but even better was to follow.

'I think it would be best up here at the cottage, if it's not
too inconvenient for you. I'll be alone here and we could talk
undisturbed. I don't – let me put it this way: I don't want to be
seen having meetings with you separately at the bank. Or in
town.'

'I see.' I didn't, but so what?

'You're very kind. I think the sooner the better. Would you be able to come tomorrow?'

This was sudden; I thought quickly. It was short notice but I could manage it. Anything that gave me more information than Jeremy had about the Carberrys was welcome. And with Liz Dennison on her own – well, who knew?

'Yes, I could.'

'If you could get here for lunch time I could rustle up something cold.' Her voice still had an invitation to it. 'Would that be all right?'

'That,' I said cheerfully, 'would be fine. About twelve-thirty, then. Tomorrow.'

'I'll look forward to that, Tim.'

'Me too, Liz.'

I put the phone down.

Sue stopped rattling and came out of the kitchenette to glare at me.

'Who was that you were talking to?' she demanded. 'Who's Liz?'

'Nobody,' I said, casually. 'Nobody at all.'

'What do you mean, nobody? It must have been someone!'

'Only business,' I said, getting up to search for strong drink. 'It's only business, Sue.'

CHAPTER 11

I went in to my office the next morning, intent on clearing up a few bits of paperwork before setting off for Cambridge. The first thing I did was to ring Chelsea Police Station and get hold of Sergeant Will Cook.

'Good morning, Mr Simpson.' His deep voice was reassuring but somehow very guarded. 'What can I do for you?'

'Have you got an inventory of Ted Murphy's shop? I'm looking for the painting he may have been going to sell me.'

'Er, we haven't taken a detailed inventory as such, no. You'd have to go to the premises and look to find – '

Cut-off: the telephone was snatched out of his hand with a thump that made the line quiver. An irritable voice took over.

'Tim? What the blazes are you about?'

Oh dear, I thought, oh dear; I should have guessed that Nobby might be in the offing, not safely immured in Scotland Yard.

'Er, hello, Nobby. How are you? You sound a bit grouchy, old friend. Not been back to Limehouse by any chance, have you?'

'Have you read the bloody papers this morning?'

'Er, no.'

'Listened to the news?'

'No, I haven't.'

'Banks has escaped.'

'Banks? You mean the villain you were celebrating about the night of the rugby thrash?'

'Yes, that one. Banks. We break our necks getting him behind bars and those bloody fools let him get away.'

'Oh dear.'

'Oh dear? Oh dear? A pathological maniac who's sworn to kill me gets out by having his mates shoot up a prison van and you say oh dear?'

'Well, I'm sorry, Nobby, but it's hardly – '

'What are you pestering Sergeant Cook for?'

'Sworn to kill you? Have you got protection?'

'Answer the bloody question!'

'Um, I was just trying to help, you know, Nobby.'

'Help? Help? In what way? I thought I told you not to interfere!'

'There's no need to be offensive, Nobby. It is a citizen's duty to advise the police of any facts which may be relevant. It's just that I had an idea about the Orpen that Ted Murphy might have been offering me. It could be a horse.'

'A horse? A horse? What the bloody hell difference does that make? What you mean is that you're bloody snooping about, trying to find it, like you bloody well always do. And get in the bloody way or cause disruption while doing it. I ought to have you charged with wasting police time.'

'Really, Nobby. The language! A troop of dragoons is what you should be in charge of, not sensitive police officers. I thought it might be of use to you in tracing his last movements, that's all. I have always understood that such things were important in piecing together this type of investigation. I realize now that I was wrong. I must have been watching too much television. *Crimewatch* and the like. I won't upset you any more. Goodbye, Nobby; do take care of yourself. And Gillian. And the kids.'

'Hey, wait a minute –'

He was too late. I put the phone down, firmly, dislodging the heap of papers I was intending to deal with.

An envelope came to my eye as I grabbed the papers to stop them sliding.

It was the one Ted Murphy's card had come in.

The postmark was Cambridge.

Cambridge.

As from a dim, far-off distance, I heard Penny, who must have come in to the office while I was staring at the postmark, addressing me.

'– lunch?'

'Sorry?'

'Claire says Jeremy says will you come to lunch with him today? There's nothing booked for you in your diary, so shall I say yes?'

'No.'

'No?'

'No.'

Postmark Cambridge. Why was that suddenly so horribly significant that it put a lump of cold fear into the bottom of my stomach?

I picked up the phone and dialled Liz Dennison's number while Penny bit her lip and rattled on.

'Tim, er, you haven't got any other appointments. I think, you know, Jeremy's trying to, well, make, um, to offer – '

'The *amende honorable*?'

Unobtainable. Not engaged. The number gave an unobtainable signal.

It hadn't yesterday.

I was getting to my feet, moving out from behind the desk. It might be just coincidence. It might not be important. There could be a fault on the line. I might just be going to have a pleasant *tête-à-tête* with a charming lady. My nerves might be completely up the spout.

'Um,' Penny said, still obviously thinking over the *amende honorable* bit, 'I think that's probably what the offer of lunch is meant to – to –'

'No chance.'

'Not? Oh, Tim. I really shouldn't say so, I know, but I really do think you ought to – Claire says Jeremy's quite upset – I mean –'

'I have a prior appointment. Near Cambridge. With Mrs Dennison.'

'Mrs Dennison?' Her jaw dropped. 'The one from yesterday?'

'Mrs Dennison. From yesterday.'

'Today?'

'Today. Lunch. I'm leaving now.'

'But, Tim –'

'Now.'

CHAPTER 12

Elizabeth Dennison's cottage was at an address out of Cambridge on a minor road beyond Fen Ditton. Fen Ditton is a place towards which, in my day, oarsmen toiled down the muddy waters of Long Reach before turning the ridiculous, right-angled bends up to Chesterton Lock, where they could rest and have a good old smoker's cough. Then they either turned round for home or hoisted the boat through for a much longer toil on the narrow, sluggish waters of the Cam.

The Jaguar went there rather faster.

Putting my foot down, I ignored the usual possibility of police cars picking up speedsters on the M11 and ignored the thought that I was going to arrive much too early for lunch. All the coincidences that have always made the hairs on the back of my neck prickle, every time I've been involved in something like this, have never turned out to be coincidences. I remembered the interested way that Elizabeth Dennison looked round my office, examined the Orpen painting of himself and Yvonne Aubicq. I remembered her curious looks at me, the intuition that told her I didn't want to buy that bloody collection. I remembered her voice, dropping to quiet tones on the phone. An arrival out of time might be a useful initiative to have taken, producing the unexpected, upsetting the prepared plan, whatever that was, that Elizabeth Dennison – or someone else – might have mapped out for me.

The conversation with Sergeant Will Cook in the Fulham Road pub came back to me forcibly, too. Would Ted Murphy's album of snaps contain one of Liz Dennison?

Why did I think of her as Liz in that context, not Elizabeth? Was Liz the all-knowing lady who could make a man sit up and take notice, as I had done, and lure him to her lair? As I shot past the aircraft museum at Duxford, I shook my head behind the wheel; my thoughts were running too fast.

I steered a long-remembered way round the northern out-skirts of Cambridge on the A45 and then doubled south along the road between Horningsea and Fen Ditton. An unmade lane described by Liz Dennison came up to my right and I took it, bumping a little on rutted tracks. The cottage came up on my left, almost down to the river bank.

There was no one there.

It was a small whitewashed building, two-storeyed, with a chimney at one end. I knocked on its front door without success. The bedroom window above the door was open, as though someone deliberately wanted to air the room, and there was a feeling of habitation. I peered in through a leaded pane to see a small living room with a television set and two chintzy arm-chairs by an open fireplace. An open door behind gave a glimpse of a kitchen.

I walked round the side of the cottage through a small hedge gap, past a dustbin and into a back garden that was secluded but small, with a bit of lawn and some flowers round it in beds. I tried knocking on the back door, then I opened it. It yawned its way outwards to show me the kitchen, neat and fairly modern, with the almost inevitable Aga stove cherished by the upper countrified classes.

'Hello!' I shouted.

No answer.

The prickles on the back of my neck had got much worse. I went in rapidly, scanned the living room, found a small, snug study with a bureau, banged my head to look into a dinky dining room. Upstairs, there were two bedrooms, both with bathrooms; Liz Dennison's guests were self-contained, when-ever they stayed. The decoration was traditional, reserved, country style. Both bedrooms had double beds. There were no photographs.

There was no one there.

I went downstairs quickly, round the other side of the house; found a small garage with a Ford Fiesta in it; definitely a woman's car with woman's bits of things in it, like a woollen scarf and, in the back seat well, a pair of scuffed women's shoes.

I went back into the kitchen, took in the surfaces with as hard a look as possible, went back into the snug study where there was a telephone, looked round and saw her handbag, or at least some woman's handbag, standing on the bureau, left

84

like no woman who was going to be absent would leave it.

She had to be here, then.

Maybe walking on the river bank?

Without a handbag? Leaving the place open?

The telephone; I picked it up, listened, heard nothing. The line was dead. Looking down, I could follow the cable to its junction, where someone had torn it out.

I quickly went back out towards my car, stared down the lane, up the lane. I walked carefully towards the river, hidden by a high hedge along the towpath, turned a leafy corner, bumped almost head-on into a big burly fellow pointing a shotgun straight at me.

A shotgun. Straight at me.

'Christ!' I shouted out loud, in shock.

Then I realized that it wasn't a shotgun. It was a bundle of fishing rods he was carrying under the crook of his arm, in a way fishermen don't normally do.

The man stared at me with a wild look. He was big, untidy, wearing old scuffed wellies. An oiled country waistcoat, stained and pocketed, sagged around his thick, stained sweater.

He couldn't be going to kill me. He didn't look right.

'For Christ's sake,' I said, 'stop pointing that thing at me.'

The fishing rods drooped. He opened his mouth. He seemed to be having trouble speaking.

'What's up?' I asked him.

'I've just seen a body.' His voice was full of horror. 'In the river.'

'Man or woman?'

'Woman,' he said.

I leapt forward to grab the fishing rods as he fainted clean away.

CHAPTER 13

'I gather,' Nobby Roberts said, coming into the interview room with heavy courtesy, 'that you and Inspector Goodall are already well acquainted?'

'What, here already?'

My sarcasm was lost on him. Since he had issued orders that I was not to be allowed to leave Cambridge City Police Station until his own arrival, and he had taken the best part of six hours to arrive, and those six hours followed rather lengthy events on the river bank near Fen Ditton, statements back at the police station, checks on their computer, calls to Scotland Yard, Chelsea and, for all I knew, the Archbishop of Canterbury, time had passed in great dollops since, together with a resuscitated fisherman, I'd found and identified the body of Elizabeth Dennison in the tangled reeds near the cottage by the Cam. Inspector Goodall and I had indeed had plenty of time to get well acquainted.

'Am I,' I demanded, 'as I have asked repeatedly over the last interminable six hours, being held here against my will on some sort of charge?'

'No, no,' Nobby said, sitting down wearily and nodding his ginger head at the offer of a cup of tea. 'You are merely helping the police with their inquiries. An activity with which you are already well acquainted. This category of retention enables us to enjoy your delightful presence for a prescribed length of time which, as I am sure you are only too aware, is by no means yet nearing its completion. By no means yet nearing its completion.'

'You are an absolute sod, do you know that, Nobby?'

'And you are an interfering, bone-headed busybody nitwit.'

'Thank you. Yes, I'll have a fifteenth cup of tea, thank you.'

Inspector Goodall of the Cambridge force raised his eyebrows at us, nodded to his WPC to bring me yet more tea in response to my last request, and sat down with us. He wasn't at all a bad

86

chap for someone patiently having to spend his days, I supposed, dealing with undergraduates in a drunken condition or taking substances they shouldn't, arresting motorists ditto, cursing at the traffic and parking problems, nicking the odd thief, bigamist and flasher, or standing to attention at university and civic processions. Bodies in the river, the sudden arrival of Scotland Yard DCIs and the like probably did not enliven life on the Fens too often. We were cheering him up no end.

'I want to hear,' Nobby said, taking the cup of tea the WPC handed him with a quick thank you, 'what the hell this is all about. In your own words.'

'I have made a statement. It has been typed on the very latest machinery. Have you read it?'

'Indeed I have. And am none the wiser.'

'But doubtless much better informed. To use F. E. Smith's immortal riposte.'

His mouth twitched. For a moment he almost grinned at me; he'd led with his jaw on that one.

'No, I am not much better informed. As with so much of what is said by you, it is what is not said that interests me most. What interests me is the between the lines, unseen information, which I believe you are withholding and which *it is a serious offence* to withhold.'

At this, Inspector Goodall nodded sagely. He was a thin bespectacled man who looked more like an accountant than a policeman, but during our hours together, on and off, we had not exactly spent the time discussing England's dreadful performance at cricket or similar trivialities; he had been extremely professional.

'I am not withholding information.'

I had had time to blot out the sickening image of the morning somewhat. The body in the reeds, clothes clinging, the wet horrid feel of slippery skin as I took a hand to turn her over and see Elizabeth Dennison's pale dead face streaked with strands of brown hair and pieces of vegetation. Mud on my trousers echoing mud down her legs. A still, inert, heavy, soggy body for a slim attractive woman with a mysterious manner. And me knowing, knowing all the way up to Fen Ditton that this was what I'd most likely find.

'When you put the phone down on me this morning –'

'This morning? Only this morning? Was that not a year ago? It bloody well feels like it was a year ago.'

'As I say, when you put the phone down on me this morning –'

'In response to your foul-mouthed injunction to poke my nose out of police business and generally to eff off –'

'Will you stop interrupting! Stop it!' He gave me a genuinely red-eyed glare, waited, then observing my silence, continued. 'When, as I say, you put the phone down on me this morning, you had just indicated that you might have been able to cast some light on the movements of the late Murphy, whose murder is being investigated by the Metropolitan force, Chelsea division.'

'I did. Or at least I might have, if you hadn't been so offensively rude.'

'In order to assist with this information, you asked if the stock at the shop had been inventoried so that you might pursue your normal greedy practice of tracking down works of art connected with criminal events in order to purchase them at a discount.'

'Well, that's rich! I –'

'Let me continue! Jesus Christ! Will you stop interrupting! You stated on the phone – I remember this distinctly – that the painting Murphy offered you, possibly of a horse, might be of use in casting some light on where he had been in the time before his death.'

'That was the gist of it, yes.'

'You then promptly and without delay drove straight up here and found the body of Mrs Dennison in the river. It has been established – Inspector Goodall here has made it quite clear to you – that she was almost certainly murdered. Hit on the head and pitched in the river. We are merely waiting a final autopsy report to confirm this.'

'Yes.'

'Yes, what? What do you mean, yes?'

'Yes, I understand it was murder. Yes, I drove up here. I did not find the body, actually. The fisherman did. Then he fainted. I went to the spot and –'

'I've read all that in your statement! What I want to know is why did you drive straight up here after putting the phone down on me?'

'I've told everyone. Mrs Dennison invited me. To lunch.'

'Lunch? Lunch? You got here before eleven. Why did she invite you?'

'Because, as I've said, she wanted to tell me something. Something that couldn't be mentioned on the phone.'

'You have no idea what it was?'

'No.'

'None?'

'No.'

'Huh! Was there any other reason why you came so quickly and urgently?'

'I have said – in detail – that the envelope for the card from Ted Murphy was postmarked Cambridge. I only found it this morning, by accident. It gave me the willies.'

'You could have told me. Or Sergeant Cook.'

'You wouldn't have connected it with Liz Dennison, would you, unless I had deliberately sicked you on to her? Hardly the friendly thing to do. I tried to call her but the number was unobtainable. For the very good reason that the line had been torn out. So, having no means of contact short of calling out the police, I shot up here as fast as I could.'

He frowned at me. 'Are you sure there was no other reason why you rushed up here to see this woman on her own?'

'What are you suggesting? That I had an assignation with her? I can assure you categorically that there was absolutely nothing *untoward* in my coming here.'

'Huh!' he said. 'I should hope not.'

'What do you mean by all this huh? She wanted, I imagine, to talk to me about the Crockingham Collection. Or – and this is what got me going – something to do with Ted. It seemed like too much of a coincidence.'

'It certainly did. Does.'

'Well, there you are.'

'There are no other facts in your possession which could have a bearing on all this?'

'None.'

'In view of the complicated, esoteric, symbolist, allegorical, one might almost say occult way, in which you and the late Murphy seem to have communicated, I suppose it would require nothing less than Jungian analysis to drag out any further possible interpretations of his message to you?'

'My goodness, Nobby, you are going it a bit, aren't you?

Anyone would think you were a product of the psychiatry faculty.'

He sighed. 'There is no point in wasting any more time. You better look in his shop with Will Cook tomorrow and we'll see if this Elizabeth Dennison features in his photograph album. You can do that for us, too. The family have been informed and they will tell her ex-husband. Inspector Goodall here has all that aspect in his capable hands and, I have no doubt, will get everyone to account for their movements. If there *is* a connection, we won't find it here tonight. I'm going back to London.'

'How are you travelling?'

He sighed again. 'Due to the escape of that bastard Banks, I am accompanied by a police driver at all times. Gillian and the kids have been moved to a safe house. I will be visiting them from time to time.'

'Gee whiz, it sounds a bit serious.'

'It is serious. Too serious for me to have to spend my time dealing with nonsensical, strong muscular hares put up by you.'

'Well, I'm sorry I keep intruding, Nobby. Surely you don't have to be divided between these two things. Isn't there someone else who can take over with one or the other?'

His face went grim. 'Banks is my pigeon and no one else's. He's sworn to get me. So are you.'

'It is a comfort, I must say, to be put in the same category as Banks.'

He didn't respond to that. He muttered something about clearing up some admin with Goodall and the two of them went out. The WPC looked at me half-sympathetically. Normally, I'd have got a male constable but I suppose because it was the murder of a woman we were dealing with, I got the opposite gender. After a while, Nobby came back with Goodall and they said I was free to go.

'So soon?'

'We will need,' Nobby said, face not responding to my heavy sarcasm, 'to maintain close vigilance. Your presence may be required at any time. Got it?'

'Feel free.'

'I'm not satisfied that we know nearly enough.'

'Nor am I.' I looked at his tired face. 'Oh, come on, Nobby, don't make me feel such a shit. At least let me buy you a consolatory pint at the Dun Cow on the old A10 road. Don't go blinding straight off back to London down the motorway. Ease up a bit.'

'I've got this driver.'

'He can either join us or follow us if you want him to. Perfect diversion for you to come in my car. Positive subterfuge; Banks would be shaken off the scent. If he were on it.'

He hesitated, then spoke out loud.

'I won't get back to Gillian tonight anyhow.'

'There you are then.' I grinned. 'I phoned Sue to say I was unavoidably detained.'

He shook his head sadly. 'OK, then. Actually you're right; I could do with a break. I'll let the driver go. You can drop me off in Chelsea.'

'Perfect.'

He seemed to cheer up after that. We briefed the driver, who was pleased to get away early. Nobby folded a very neat mobile phone into his side pocket. Watching him, a thought occurred to me.

'I say, are you armed, Nobby?'

'Oh, yes.'

I looked at him. His clothes seemed perfectly normal. Nobby is quite a dab hand with a police revolver, so there was no need to worry about being accosted, not that I thought that there was any chance of that. We set off in my Jaguar down the old A10 and after a village or so, the Dun Cow came up in front of us. We were soon parked behind a table with pints in hand.

'Now, you tell me,' he said, after a long pull had gone down, 'how Mrs Dennison, sorry, the late Mrs Dennison, née Carberry, could come to be mixed up with Ted Murphy, an Orpen painting – possibly of a horse – and anything else you can think of.'

'I can't, except that Ted Murphy seems to have been a ladies' man and she was divorced. I hadn't even taken in the fact that Orpen had ever painted a horse in my recollection; it's not a subject I associate with him. If it hadn't been for Mr Goodston, the entire idea would never have occurred to me. But Mr Goodston said he'd seen Murphy at Newmarket. The card was posted in Cambridge. Why? Did he just post it on his way home? Or had he been at Fen Ditton? I just had all these questions in my mind; too many coincidences crowding together, so I set off.'

'You have no idea what she might have been going to tell you?'

'I assumed it was something about the purchase of the Collection. Then I remembered the way she looked at my painting in the office. She also asked her brother if they hadn't had an Orpen once, or at least if her father had, and he said, no, Orpen didn't paint horses. He was dead wrong there for a start.'

'It's all very tenuous, Tim. You get a card with a Bugatti or two on it and in no time you're chasing phantom horses painted by artists who didn't paint them. Or, at least, weren't noted for it.' He cocked his head to look at me askance. 'I wonder if you'll ever be able to resist the temptation? There's a bit of you that's never grown up, isn't there?'

'Thank God it hasn't. If getting too bloody bored or too bloody tired to be excited about anything is called growing up, why bother? What's there to grow up for?'

He chuckled. 'Don't get all stroppy, Tim. I like the way there are certain gaps in your maturity. It helps to think of you as an eternal Peter Pan. Even though you drive me mad when you get these bees in your bonnet.'

This in turn made me smile. Nobby became a policeman out of a strong sense of social morality. Even after years of what must be frustrating, disillusioning, wearying compromise with the realities of the law, the politics of the service and the worst aspects of human nature, he has retained that moral clarity, that initial enthusiasm for putting things right, which he started with. Which makes him just as much an innocent, a Peter Pan, as anyone I know.

'You could have fooled me,' I riposted. 'The way you and your rozzers carry on, you'd think I was a major villain instead of the source of all these solutions for you.'

He affected to choke on his beer. 'Solutions? You? If I had to reach the solution the way you do in most cases, I'd be in the loony bin by now and my men would have resigned *en masse*. Everything is always so convoluted.' He paused thoughtfully and peered into his glass as though the convolutions could be deconvoluted by its crystal-ball clarity; Nobby never leaves work alone. 'Murphy couldn't have meant something else, by any chance, could he?'

'I suppose he could. But I can't think what. Another pint might help.'

'It might. Even if it doesn't, it'll certainly help everything else. It's been a strain down at Chelsea today, I can tell you.'

'Chelsea? I thought you were chasing this maniac Banks.'

'I am. Banks is a resident of the borough, Tim. He's not an East End mobster. The operation is centred on Chelsea nick.'

'You devil! All the time it's been quite convenient for you to cover both cases. And I thought you were running like a hare.'

I stared at him in genuine indignation; he always puts on such a pained martyr's personality when it comes to these things.

He grinned. 'I don't have to make you feel anything's easy, do I? You'd never let up if I did.'

'You rotten bugger! You can stand this round for that.'

'My pleasure.' He paused as he stood up and gestured at my glass. 'Quite happy about driving, are you?'

'Two pints won't put me over the limit.'

His face puckered. 'You can't be too careful, Tim. This is strong stuff. Tell you what: I'll have a half and I'll drive us back. I've always wanted to have a go at that Jag of yours.'

Nobby is a good driver, advanced police course, all that stuff. I nodded cheerfully. 'It'll be a pleasure to have a police chauffeur. The least you could do after today. Nothing over a hundred and thirty, though.'

He pulled a face. When he came back, one pint and one half in hand, he looked at me curiously. 'Did you want to buy the Crockingham Collection, by the way? Was that your idea?'

I took my glass. 'Nope. I'm not much keen on it, except for the Munnings. Jeremy and Sir Richard think they're killing two birds with one stone.'

'Oh?'

'Discreetly acquiring a so-called important collection and helping a client in difficulties. The Carberrys are in deep Lloyds, as we say nowadays.'

'So Carberry is an important client?'

'Oh, yes.'

'Mmm.'

'What does mmm mean?'

'It means that my lips should be sealed. But Sir Andrew Carberry came very close once, very close.'

'What, during your days on the Fraud Squad?'

'Shh.' He put a finger to his lips. 'It was a close-run thing, as the great Duke said. Very close. But nothing was done. So – Sir Andrew being notoriously litigious – one says nothing defamatory. Made his money in the wholesale grocery business originally. Cash and carry. Including vegetables. Knight of the shires now, of course. Industrial interests, printing, you name it.'

'Yes, I know all that, Nobby. All horses and plummy tones. Quite the country gentleman. Not a gentle man, though. He made me go to the tradesman's entrance, which is a laugh. But what was he up to?'

'Most of the things you *can* get up to. Treatment of perishables is very important in the vegetable and grocery trade. He knocked a lot out for cash. Fiddled his stock write-offs.' Nobby made a broad, sweeping gesture. 'Disposals of assets. Depreciations. All very difficult to prove. Treated publicly-quoted companies as though they were his own possessions. Usual thing.'

'Ah. Thanks for the tip-off. Jeremy and Sir Richard are rather protective of Sir Andrew and family. Don't want me to rock the boat. Nervous of losing his custom, you might say.'

'Maxwell relied on much the same thing.' He put down his glass. 'We better go, Tim. It's getting late.'

'You're telling me?'

I swallowed the rest of my pint, gave him my keys and we sauntered out into the gloom of the pub car park. He went to the driver's door, presented the right key, and paused.

'Ah. I have to remember to practise my security procedures.'

'Oh really? Do you have to practise now?'

'Yes, I do. The trainer is an ex-Belfast man. He gave me a rigorous session on this. The important thing is to develop the right habits and stick to them all the time.' He put his head up. 'First, look round generally; no obvious dangers?'

'Not that I can see. No men in Balaclavas skulking in the doorway of the Gents with their violin cases, anyway.'

He ignored that. 'Car is out on its own. Is it apparently clear externally?'

'Yes.'

'But parked where access is very easy?'

'True.'

'So, before putting key into lock, do external check. Then look underneath.'

'Banks is a bomber, is he? Chelsea via the Falls Road? Pockets full of gelly, available for the spontaneous occasion, the im-promptu detonation?'

'Banks will kill by any method he thinks possible. Banks should be in Rampton, not a normal gaol, but that's not what happens.'

He stooped, went down gently on one knee and peered under the car. I couldn't help smiling.

'You can't see a bloody thing in this light, Nobby.'

'Which is why' – he put his hand in his pocket and pulled it out again with a small cylinder in it – 'I carry this special torch.'

'Brill!'

'With this torch I look under the petrol tank, axles, front seat area –'

His voice stopped strangely, half muffled by the vehicle side.

'What's up? Found a dead skunk?'

His voice was still muffled, booming under the bodywork. 'Stand away from the car.'

'Eh?'

He came upright slowly, carefully, face distorted.

'I said stand away from the bloody car, Tim! Now!'

I stood away. In fact, I bounded about four paces in less than a split second. His tones were compulsive to obedience. My hair began to rise on end slowly in a sort of delayed-action stupidity.

He now stepped back, too, about five cautious paces. His face was still twisted. 'There's a bloody bomb under the front seats. Right plumb centre!'

'Jesus Christ!' I heard my words as hoarse and incredulous. 'No, come off it, Nobby, there can't be. I don't believe this. Are you sure?'

'It's attached to the transmission.' He was scanning the car park quickly, looking at the other vehicles, but we were quite alone.

Reaction hit me. 'Look, this isn't just some clever training exercise is it? Because if it is, I'm not going to be very –'

'No, it isn't!' He cut me short. 'It's unmistakable. I can't tell whether it's wired or not. I mean, whether it's set off by movement, by remote control or even ignition. It could even be on a timer, like a clock of some sort.'

Now I found myself really agitated. 'Look, bugger the bloody technicalities, Nobby, I mean, Christ, hadn't we better scarper –'

But he already had his mobile phone out and was dialling, thumping the buttons with spiked fingers.

Set off by remote control? I started to look round nervously. If someone could see us, he might decide to detonate, now that his bomb was discovered.

Nobby spoke to me across the distance with his phone clapped to his ear. 'If anyone comes out of the pub, for God's sake keep them well away from here. For the moment. We'll have to cordon the area off – no, wait, go into the pub and clear the whole of this side of the building. Everybody over to the other side.' He started gabbling into the mobile phone then looked up to see me still frozen to the tarmac. I couldn't believe it; this wasn't happening.

'What if it's a timer?'

'What if it's a timer? It'll go off when the timer makes it, that's what! Go on! Don't just bloody well stand there, Tim; make yourself bloody useful for a change!'

I ran into the pub, mouthing oaths. It's just like Nobby to berate me like that, even when the fault's his for once.

I mean, this was beyond me, this sort of thing. The people I have to deal with in the art trade don't use bombs. They can't, for obvious reasons.

Unless it's for insurance purposes, of course. Almost anything goes when it's for insurance purposes.

I burst into the saloon bar, trying not to bellow out loud in sheer bloody terror.

CHAPTER 14

Sue watched me traipse wearily out of the bedroom in my bath-robe, snap the kettle switch back on, put some Imperial Blend into the pot, pick up the boiling vessel and bung the steaming water on to the bags within. Stubble bristled around my chin as the vapour moistened it. Grit gritted under my eyelids.

'So,' she said, in mock-statement mode, 'you went back up to Cambridge for the day, yesterday.'

'Yes.' I trailed back across the room holding the teapot and sat grumpily at the table. She'd finished her cereal and had been sipping coffee. It hadn't been a good night for her, either.

'And you found a murdered woman's body in the river, whereas Nobby, who came up to join you for a couple of beers, merely found a live bomb under your car?'

'You have yet again summarized the day's events succinctly, Sue.'

'Was that all?'

'That,' I said tetchily, 'was quite enough.'

'And the body was that of the mysterious Liz you wouldn't tell me about, but who you were obviously keen to see.'

'It was.'

'Only business, I think you said.'

'Only business.' I put two pieces of white bread in the toaster, located a block of butter, peered about for the marmalade. My gritty eyes were bunged up. I had got home very late the night before. No, correction: the same morning. The police car that had kindly brought me back had carried Nobby on to Chelsea, still mouthing oaths about what he would do to Banks once he caught him. My car was a lost cause. Forensic men of all sorts, once the bomb had been defused, wanted to play with the vehicle, possibly dismantle substantial parts of it. I doubted if I'd see it again this side of Christmas. I felt knackered.

'Some business this lady was in.'

'Have you seen the marmalade?'

'It is on the table in front of you. In the amber jar.'

I managed to focus. 'Amber jar? How long have we had that?'

'Since your Aunt Daisy gave it to us as a wedding present. And this Liz is – was – a Carberry, was she?'

'She was. As I think I have already explained. An important one. Sister to Philip and James. Daughter to Sir Andrew. Why is the marmalade in an amber jar with a little lid which is ridiculous? Who did that?'

'Guess. I was sick of seeing the pot on the table.'

'I shall never be able to find it, now.'

'Tim! For God's sake will you stop trying to be flippant and answer me! What the hell is going on?'

'I told you last night.'

'I haven't slept a wink. You haven't told me anything.'

The toast popped up and I put it in the rack to cool before getting the butter to it, scowling the while at the amber jar.

'I don't agree with marmalade being hidden like that.'

'*Tim!*'

'I'm sorry. There's something about these events that brings out the worst in me. The most sardonic, I mean. It's some sort of defence mechanism. The alternative would be to start throwing up at the memory of that body and go on throwing up until I collapsed. Or have nightmares. Well, I do have nightmares from time to time, as you know. Shell shock, it used to be called. Comes of brooding on things. I mean, if Nobby hadn't done his little security drill like the well-trained rozzer he is, that would have been that. Bits of Timmy raining down all over the Fens. Fortunately, the bank has excellent pension and widow's benefits. All fully paid up.'

'Tim, stop it! Please stop it!'

'Well, what do you want me to do? Burst into bloody tears?'

I was sorry I said that. Her eyes were suddenly full of tears. Tears of both anger and fear. I got up, went round the table and put my arms round her, feeling bad. She grabbed a tissue from somewhere and made snorting noises into it. Sue is tough most of the time and it blinds me to the softness underneath. When the surface cracks, the vulnerability comes as a terrible shock. It's my own fault.

'I'm sorry. I'm really very sorry. I had no idea you'd be so upset. It wasn't meant for me, you know. It was Nobby they were after.'

'But it could have been you! And that poor woman; suppose you'd come across the – the murderer – at the wrong time?'

'I can look after myself, Sue.'

'You always say that. You won't leave things alone. Then you nearly always get terribly hurt. I don't know how it happens. First this man Murphy and now the Carberry woman. It's not as though it'll stop, is it?'

'God, I hope it will. I don't know what it's about, but surely it can't go on. Not with two lots of policemen after it. Maybe it's the ex-husband, Dennison. Jealousy. Or a boyfriend of Elizabeth Dennison's. Or something like that.'

'Well, I hope to God it is. And I hope to God for Gillian's sake, as well as for ours, that they catch this terrible man Banks as soon as possible.'

'They will now. You can't try to blow up the rozzers in England and think you'll get very far. Take it very personally, they do. Nobby was in a rare old rage and so were his men. I expect all those East End gangsters will help to shop Banks in some way after this. They get very nervy about outsiders like Banks; don't like them at all. Mind you, I was dead unpopular too, as usual. They nearly asked me to walk home.'

'You?' Indignation filled her voice. 'Why you? It wasn't your fault.'

'Ah, but I had persuaded Nobby, in a moment of weakness, to abandon his police car and set off all unguarded, hadn't I? For a loose, beer-drinking evening. At least that was the implication. I could tell that Nobby felt he'd blundered. Some senior officer is going to give him a wigging, you bet. So will Gillian, for sure, when she hears about it. If I hadn't been there, the argument will run, the opportunity wouldn't have arisen. The detective chief inspector showed uncharacteristic weakness. Exposed himself unnecessarily. *Ergo*, I'm to blame. A bad influence. My policy right now is to lie low, do as I'm told and cooperate with the force. Which is why I've got up when everything about me wants to stay in bed. I have to meet Sergeant Will Cook down at the Fulham Road.'

She nodded understandingly. She seemed to have recovered a bit; I went back to my seat, buttered a piece of toast, looked for the marmalade, remembered the amber jar, took its bloody silly little lid off, and spooned out some orange and grapefruit marmalade. Sue poured herself a little more coffee.

'Tim, Mary phoned me yesterday.'

'Oh?' Mary is Jeremy's wife. She and Sue are very thick.

'She said Jeremy was quite upset that you wouldn't go to lunch with him.'

'Couldn't, Sue, not wouldn't. I had to go to Cambridge.'

'I know. That's what I told her was probably the case. Anyway, she says she hopes you won't avoid him again today. So I thought I'd better tell you; look out for another lunch invitation. And accept it if you can.'

'I'll be there,' I said, heavily.

'You know I hate it when you and Jeremy get at odds.'

'Oh? Only two days ago you said I should resign because the bugger is absolutely impossible.'

'He is. But I was upset, then. I should hate us all to fall out and not see Mary again.'

I opened my mouth, paused, then bit quickly into the toast. I decided I was not going to comment. Comment would have been quite superfluous and almost certainly contentious.

An hour later, I headed down to the Fulham Road by taxi, feeling a bit restored by a hot bath and clean shirting. Sergeant Will Cook was waiting outside the door of Ted Murphy's shop-cum-gallery, looking as stocky and dependable as before. He had a parcel under his arm.

'Well, well, well,' he said, putting on his best drama-policeman act as he gave me a quick shake of the hand, 'we have been a busy little bee, haven't we?'

I grinned at him. 'You've seen Nobby recently, I assume.'

'Seen? Recently? I have had him, along with the entire staff of the nick, shouting into my shell-like all night! Taken it very personally, he has. Action stations for everyone.' Cook smiled back at me. 'Don't blame him, mind, but it's hard on the rest of the crew. The whole nick has been stampeding around like a herd of buffaloes. Like John Wayne's last round-up, it was, last night. Ground all churned up and turds everywhere.'

'Oh dear.'

'Oh dear is putting it very delicately, so to speak. Tell me, by the way: when you're not sending messages to murdered men, is it your normal practice to shoot off and locate murdered women in the depths of rivers?'

'Now then, Will. May I call you Will?'

'You certainly may, Tim. I'm just curious as to how it's done, that's all. I mean, I could base my career on just hanging round Onslow Gardens and following you, could I?'

I grinned. 'That's what Nobby's had to do. Doesn't seem to appreciate the opportunities, though.'

'Well, don't be too sure. Although he's a bit raw about setting himself up as a target like that. In your car, I mean. Even if it was for the best of intentions. Anyway, come on, we'll open up and let the dog see the rabbit.'

I raised my eyebrows but he was already jangling a set of keys. In no time the door was open and in we went.

Ted Murphy's place was really a large shop adapted to the needs of the paintings and antiques he traded in. There were spotlights in rails on the ceiling and the light-coloured walls were neutral, originally kept fairly clear so that canvases could be better displayed. Encroachment, however, had cluttered the desired effect; the stock, some of it long-serving, was gradually silting up the clean, gallery atmosphere Ted had originally wanted to convey. There was an area of furniture and bric-à-brac of an artistic nature – Ted was into Art Nouveau quite a bit – which currently looked quite full. Odd things, including a North Country longcase clock and a quaint standard lamp, intruded on to the wall space. A big splashy watercolour with a cracked glass and oversized frame, depicting a country scene with two shire horses interminably ploughing a brown field while a weary ploughman plodded behind them, hung over his desk on the opposite wall where I had seen it hang, to my knowledge, for nearly two years. I could never work out why Ted didn't knock the awful thing out at auction, but he said it had its uses; its dark mount made it suitable to use as a mirror to adjust his tie in and the subject made all the other paintings look so much better. I thought that it gave an impression of terrible taste, but Ted said you couldn't bank on that; some of his customers liked it but wouldn't pay the money. It'll go one day, he said, for what I've got to get for it.

Looking round now, seeing the dust collected and collecting, the impression of Ted's lack of success came to me even more strongly. His mind could never specialize the way it should have. He was too intellectually curious for that. The general dealer now effectively runs a junk shop; all the successful boys, in the teeth of auctioneering success, have become specialists of some sort.

'Well,' Will Cook said. 'This is it. Have a good look. See if your horse or Bugatti or nude lady or whatever is here. There's a stack of paintings against that wall over there.'

'Right.' I moved further into the place, scanning the walls. I didn't expect there'd be an Orpen hung up there, and there wasn't. There was a gluey Mellor of the Lake District in the rain; there was a Russell 'Tits' Flint signed print of Spanish ladies at a well, boldly baring large, firm, pre-silicone age bosoms that were far too good to be true, as though that was how Spanish ladies always collected buckets of water; there was a Dixon watercolour of the Pool of London with regulation tramp steamer, Thames barge and tea clipper looking a bit faded behind its glass; a watercolour of a woman feeding chickens outside a thatched cottage surrounded by twenty-four varieties of flowers, possibly by one of the many, many Stannards or Strachan or one of those; there was a de Breanski of a pink sun setting on rocky Scottish mountains above a loch fringed with pines. There was also an unsigned oil of peonies in a vase. That completed what you might call the Period Wall. Ted had these to keep up his turnover; his heart was not in them but they were saleable. I turned my attention to the moderns, opposite.

There wasn't an Orpen there, either.

There was a marvellous Nicholson print and there was a bad Augustus John of two women with ewers on their heads and a William Rothenstein, not so usual, that, and some excellent small Slade School ladies and a Duncan Grant still life and even a Terrick Williams of a Breton harbour and a Meninsky of a bowl of fruit, but there was no Orpen. I went to the stack of paintings leaning against the wall and went through them quickly but they were minor stuff that Ted put there deliberately for people to comb through in hopes of finding a bargain; quite a lot of paintings sell well that way. I went round the rest of the place, looked at the desk with the telephone and old answering machine on its still-littered surface, felt a pang, peered into the drawers, shook my head to Will Cook.

'Upstairs to the flat, then,' he said. 'And you can look at the ladies.'

He held up the parcel he was carrying and we went outside, locking the door. The entrance to the flat was separate, on the left, and he unlocked that so we could go in, up the narrow stairway, on to a landing on the first floor and then into the front room, which was the living room. I looked round its walls too. There wasn't an Orpen there either.

But there was a Munnings.

I had never seen it before. It was a small painting of a paddock with a horse in the foreground and another horse half-sketched in behind. It was not a finished painting; the trees round the paddock were stroked in quickly with bold lines like an Impressionist might have done. The effect was arresting, livelier than a finished work might have been; oil sketches are often like that. If you've seen Constable's preparatory paint sketches, done on the spot before he took them back to his studio to work up into a finished painting by artificial light, you might have the same feeling. They are much more dynamic, brilliant, gripping than a great deal of the finished work. This was the man in action, scrabbling it down then and there, straight from the life. With someone having the talent of Constable – or Munnings – the immediacy is fantastic.

'I didn't know he'd got a Munnings,' I murmured.

'Sorry?'

'It's a Munnings. This small painting here.'

'Oh?' Sergeant Will Cook came over to look at it. 'Is it important?'

The more finished horse was brown with one semi-white forefoot and two white back socks up to the ankles. It had a bridle on and was looking down ruminatively at the ground, whereas the other horse, also a brown one, looked straight ahead. Behind them, apart from the trees, was a vague outline of buildings, a tower, possibly a stable. It was signed in one corner.

'Nice,' said Cook. He looked round the room, his attention wandering. 'Have you seen anything likely at all?'

I pulled my attention away from the horse sketch. 'Sorry. I'm sure you need to get on. No, I haven't. I'll do the rest of the flat.'

It didn't take me long. There was no sign of anything 'likely', as Cook put it. No Orpen anywhere.

'Pity,' he said. 'But it was worth trying. Cover every possibility, that's police work. Now let's show you the ladies.'

He unwrapped the parcel and carefully took out two albums,

the usual commercial sort, putting one down on the living room table in front of me.

'Go through that carefully,' he said. 'Take your time. There's not so many, so look at each one for as long as you need.'

He opened the cover and I stared at the first page. To me, it has always seemed tragic to find photograph albums in junk shops. They occur more and more frequently nowadays because people know there is historical merit in quite a few of the scenes. But usually what you get is the normal, fond progression of family albums: the weddings, parties, children, outings, dogs, gardens, laughter. It is a terrible intrusion, as though you have stolen part of someone's life. You realize how temporary it is, how transitory, how quickly it's all over. Photograph albums are too poignant for me.

This one was different. The first page already looked dated, with black and white snaps from what must have been a simple 35-millimetre camera of twenty or twenty-five years ago. The four separate girls were in their late teens and smiled shyly or grinned at the camera on their own. They wore flower-printed dresses or blouses and skirts. I turned the page. There were pictures of two girls aged about seventeen on a seaside pier, holding hands. Both wore shorts. Then they had posed separately. Opposite, they were in bathing suits. I turned another page. Now there was colour as well as black and white. A girl in a garden, sitting in a deck chair, showing a lot of leg. She'd be in her twenties, though, not a teenager. More pictures of her overleaf, in different places: Brighton, Trafalgar Square, hot sunshine on the Mediterranean somewhere, Spain perhaps. A steady, obviously.

'"Too much confectionery, too rich,"' I quoted, '"I choke on such nutritious images."'

'Pardon?'

'Sorry. Philip Larkin. Lines on a young lady's photograph album.'

'Oh.' Cook sounded mystified.

'A poem.'

'Oh.'

More modern scenes as I went on. A dark girl, a blonde. The Fulham Road; the shop with a woman in her thirties standing outside. I flicked back. It was the same girl as the 'steady', the one in the garden. On the next page, bigger prints of two girls at a table, a café overlooking the sea. Then a well-dressed blonde at the Portobello Road, with stalls in the background draped with silver pots.

'She looks American,' I said.

'Mmm?' Cook moved to peer over my shoulder. 'Her? You think so? Why?'

'The clothes.'

'Oh.' He didn't dissent with me. 'She's in the other album, that one. I'll show you after.'

I paged on. Not many more to go. The ladies were now mostly in their thirties but there were still one or two younger ones. Ted's girlfriends matured with him. The photography was much better, more sophistication coming into the composition. It was all colour, now. The faces were much better shown. Character came through them more clearly than with the earlier black and whites. The development of the prints was more sophisticated, too.

'I wonder where he got these done,' I said.

Cook pointed to the ceiling. 'I haven't taken you upstairs yet. He'd got a dark room in the attic. There's just space enough up there.'

'Good heavens! Ted was literally a dark horse. I'd no idea he was a photo freak.'

'Seen anything yet?'

I shook my head, closing the album. 'There's no sign of Liz Dennison in this lot.'

'Right. Pity. Now for the other one. You might want to sit down.'

'Oh? Why?'

'These are a bit raw, so to speak.' His expression went knowing. 'This is what you might call the private album.'

I took the second album and opened it. The first page had a print almost the same size as the page. It was a black and white nude, quite modest, with raised knee but otherwise completely revealing. The girl was young and very photogenic. Russell Flint would have been pleased to paint her bosoms. I didn't recall her from the other album.

'His first,' Cook said, watching me. 'She was a good one to start with. He went on from there, though.'

I turned the pages. Some of the girls were from the other album; the 'steady' girl started to appear in more and more provocative poses. Then there was one of her bending over the very table I was sitting at. I turned the page, feeling hot.

'Christ!' I said, as the next image came up.

'That's the Portobello one.' Will Cook's voice was matter-of-fact. 'The one you thought was American.'

'And that's Ted.'

'We think he either used a timer or else the camera was hidden. The hidden theory is the most likely. These next are all taken in the back bedroom. A timer would have been difficult, if you think about it. He'd have to get the girl all set up, nip off, prime the camera and nip back on again, despite the interruption, and still be able to – to be – er – to be –'

'In that position?'

'That's right.' His voice was still matter-of-fact. I suppose CID men are hardened to most things. But I'd known Ted. And this was him, this now-dead, obscene figure entangled with the Portobello girl. I felt hotter. I didn't want to go on with this.

Cook spoke again. 'I certainly think the camera was hidden. Behind his dressing table. There are marks in the wood – a clamp or something – which look likely. There are too many for them all to have agreed to this sort of caper.' He sounded thoughtful. 'Girls of a certain sort will do this sort of thing knowingly. Even some married women, in my experience. But for most it's too risky. Or upsetting.'

'Hell!'

'Shocks you, doesn't it? It's not like a magazine from a Soho porn shop, is it? When it's someone you know, I mean.'

'Yes. It does.'

'Sorry about it. But we need to know.'

I turned the pages. If anything, they got worse. But Will Cook was probably right. Most of the photos were taken from the same angle, the same place. The faces were always visible, whether in the repose of satiation or distorted with passion. Ted had liked variety, that was clear. Variety of women and variety of activity, always with more light than I believed most people would find natural, but this presumably was to do with the photography.

'Could he,' I asked after a few moments, closing the album, 'have set up a switch on or in the bed – or at the side of it – and pressed it when he wanted a particular shot? Especially with the face in view?'

'He might very well have. I've talked to our photo boys. They say that's easy.'

I thought of them down at the police station looking, possibly laughing, the ribald remarks. I wasn't up to this. I put the album down, feeling myself sweating even more. A metallic tinge had got into my saliva.

'I can't go on. I knew him, you see. I mean, I didn't know about this. I don't want to know about this. Not any more of it.'

'Please look at all of them.' Cook sounded like a nurse administering nasty medicine to a nauseous child. 'Then it can be finished and eliminated. Try to identify anyone if you possibly can. It's very important.'

I forced myself somehow to stifle my feelings. I went back to the photographs. Romanticists might, in literature, refer to these naked grapplings as arabesques or some such artistic euphemism. At the rugby club they'd use much coarser, more graphic language. Why the legs cranked like that, or crossed like those? And that; my gorge rose at that. It wasn't Ted any more, or maybe the effect of turning the pages was to deaden any feeling I had for him. The human system's defences overtook me. Now the pictures became clinical, grainy, unpleasant views of animal life. The two distant, porcine bodies in them, in these ridiculous postures, looked like – what was it? – 'the victims of some terrible accident, clumsily engaged, as if in some incoherent experimental fashion they were the first partners in the history of the human race to think out this peculiar means of communication.'

Except that this was not Lawrence Durrell's Alexandria, this was a blowsy bedroom over an antique shop and art gallery in the Fulham Road; and that was Ted Murphy who I had liked and with whom I had discussed not just the art of fifty years but other things; some of them serious and philosophical, some of them funny and delightful, during the time that he had been engaging in this tragic and ludicrous treachery.

I suppose I should have laughed tolerantly at it.

I hated it.

'No,' I said, snapping the bloody volume shut. 'No, no, no! There is no Elizabeth Dennison there.'

'You're sure? You look upset. Try to be calm. Please be absolutely sure. It can be difficult, obviously.'

107

'I'm sure. Really I am.'

'If there is any doubt you should look again.'

'There's no doubt. She's not in there, thank God. It's enough that she should have to suffer the shame of murder, the river, post-mortems, without being included in this. I want to get out.'

'I understand.'

'Some of those faces will never go away.'

Will Cook shook his head. 'That's what I used to say. But they'll go. You'll see; they'll go.'

I stared at the album, mercifully closed on its implacable images. 'He was a blackmailer, was he?'

'We don't know. So far there's no evidence of that. Not from his bank accounts. But there may be other bank accounts, deposits, we don't know of.'

'And these – unfortunate women? I suppose you'll trace them, will you?'

He nodded slowly. 'We will certainly have to try. It'll take a long time, though, and some may never be identified. We're not just a bunch of clumsy flatfoots, Tim. We do have some delicacy. The girlfriend who was pretty steady has already been found and interviewed. She lives in Wales now, has been married for six years and has two children. Her husband knows nothing about this and we've checked where he was the night of the murder. He couldn't possibly have done it. That's police work, you know; tedious and painstaking and usually boring, but necessary. Gradually, we'll eliminate most of them, one after the other, until the right situation comes up. But we won't find all of them unless we're very lucky.' He sighed. 'So the Dennison murder looks unconnected. From these albums, anyway.'

'Yes.'

'And you've no idea what he might have been doing in the Cambridge area?'

'No.'

He stood up, parcelled the two albums up again carefully, and gestured at the landing. 'You want to go. I understand. Pity it's a blank. Come on, I'll lock up.'

'Sure.' I took one more look round the room, saw the Munnings again, wondered where he got it, how long he'd had it, whether it was connected, wagged my head slowly. Too many other images were crowding out the rural idyll of relaxed horses. I'd have to think about that later.

'Can I give you a lift anywhere?'

I shook my head. 'I need some fresh air. Badly. I'll walk for a bit.'

'Where are you going?'

'Back to the bank. Work, like life, has to go on.'

'You'll feel better outside.'

His face was sympathetic and I was sorry in one way that I'd not done much to help so far. But I walked for a long time and breathed quite a lot of air, most of it not very fresh, before I got back to work.

CHAPTER 15

'Thank heavens!' Penny said, as I walked past her to the door of my office. 'I was beginning to wonder.'

She didn't just trail in after me, she nipped in pretty smartish before I could close the door.

''Morning, Penny.'

She shot a quick look at the desk clock to check and said, 'Good afternoon, Tim.'

'Don't be both technical and pedantic, Penny. You're too young for that. It may be after noon but it's not lunch time yet.'

'Jeremy wants to know –'

'If lunch is what he's offering, the answer is yes.'

She grabbed the phone on my desk, standing her ground, and dialled to tell Claire the good news. I sat down and contemplated the paperwork that had built up in front of me. The Art Fund is by no means my only responsibility and some of the faxes, I could see, were getting querulous. Injured tones and acerbic phrases were being employed.

'Sir Andrew Carberry rang for you.' Penny, having told Claire that I was at last receptive, put the phone down and consulted her pad. 'He wants you to phone him, urgently.'

'Ah. Does he?'

'Yes. He was pretty brisk. Shall I phone and connect you now?'

'No.'

'No?'

'No. Go to the *Art Sales Index* over there and look up Orpen for me.'

'But Tim –'

'Orpen! "Sergeant Murphy". Now.'

She almost glared at me. 'What?'

'I want you,' I said, using my calmest, most civil, and patient tones, 'to go to the *Art Sales Index* like a good girl and look up, under Orpen, that is Sir William Orpen RA, the price paid for any painting of his with the title "Sergeant Murphy". Now.'

'But when – I mean, what year?' The message was getting through; she moved over to the shelves as she asked the question.

'Start at the latest volume and work backwards.'

'How far?'

'Ten or twelve years should do it. It won't take you long.'

'If you say so.'

I picked up the phone as she started to take the first L to Z volume down and dialled Crockingham Hall. After a skirmish with a female hussar of some sort I was put through to the heavy dragoon.

'Simpson?' The voice was peremptory; wasps on plum jam.

'Good morning, Sir Andrew.'

'Good afternoon. Don't get to your offices early do you, you fellows?'

I let that one ride. After a pause, I said, 'I am very sorry about the news concerning your daughter, Mrs Dennison, Sir Andrew. A dreadful business.'

'Yes.' For a moment I felt sorry; the note had gone gruff. More of a bumblebee than a wasp. 'It's been a terrible knock, Simpson. She was my only daughter, you know.'

'I'm very sorry, Sir Andrew. I only met her once, but I thought she had a most attractive and impressive character.'

'Yes, well; that's what I wanted to speak to you about. I understand you found her?'

'Not quite, Sir Andrew.' I can be as pedantic as the next man when it suits. 'She was found by a fisherman. I happened to arrive at that time and called the police.'

'You arrived at that time.' He repeated it as though he were a barrister in cross-examination. 'May I ask how you came to be there?'

'At Mrs Dennison's request, Sir Andrew.'

'My daughter's request? You? What for?'

He must, I thought to myself, have had a good time to absorb the information, but he's acting as though it's new to him. He doesn't like the possibilities; James will have told him about being here in my office, but James won't be able to explain how I came to be speeding up to Fen Ditton the morning after.

'At Mrs Dennison's request, Sir Andrew.'

'I heard you the first time. What for?'

'I'm afraid Mrs Dennison didn't say on the phone. She asked me to see her in confidence and asked if we could meet at Fen Ditton. I agreed to go to see her yesterday.'

'In confidence? At the cottage?'

'Yes, Sir Andrew.'

'Why, Simpson?'

His voice had thickened. Proprietorial anger had seeped into the clogged throat. At the bookshelves, Penny let out a strangled exclamation, diverting my attention, then bent her head in concentration again.

'Simpson? I'm waiting.' The voice sharp, now. He was getting peremptory.

'I have no idea why.' I was getting a bit pissed off with this bully, even though I was still sorry for him. 'She didn't say. Something she didn't want to talk about on the phone.'

And you, I thought, should be damn grateful to me for looking through those horrendous photos of Ted's in order to eliminate her from something that would give you apoplexy if you'd known what I'd thought was possible.

'You must agree,' Carberry's voice was more measured, but still not pleasant, 'that it seems strange that within half a day of meeting you at your office, *you say* that she asked you to come to Cambridge.'

'Does it?'

'Don't be impudent with me, Simpson! I'm not mincing my words! I find it damned odd and I don't think I like it. Our communications are with Richard and Jeremy, not with some junior snoop from the Art Fund who goes sniffing round where he's no business to be. And says that he found the body of my daughter in very suspicious circumstances.'

'The death of your daughter is very distressing, Sir Andrew. When you are in a calmer frame of mind I am sure you will realize that there is no cause for misgivings on your part about my presence at Fen Ditton.'

'Oh, I will, will I? You're holding back something, Simpson! You're not telling the whole story, are you?'

'There is no more to what you call the story than what I have told you.'

'I'll have to have a word with the Whites about this!'

He's damned defensive, I thought; what's he hiding? Or does

112

he really think I nipped up there with a view to more intimate acquaintance? Was she perhaps inclined to quick pick-ups of that sort?

'I'm afraid that will not alter matters, Sir Andrew.'

'Oh, won't it? You'll be hearing more about this.' The voice rasped unpleasantly, then the receiver went down. I replaced mine and looked at Penny, whose ears had been flapping madly at the same time as her pen had been scribbling. The volumes had been in and out of the shelves in rapid, nimble succession.

'I've gone back as far as 1972,' she said, almost breathless.

'That's a quick twenty years. I can see you're getting the hang of this.'

'It's called "Sergeant Murphy and Things", not just "Sergeant Murphy".' Her face was triumphant at the correction.

'Really? I wonder why.'

She shook her head. 'I don't know. It sold at Sotheby's in 1972 for £2,000.'

'Well done! That's much further back than I asked.'

'Then Christie's in 1980. £9,091, it fetched then.'

'Eight years and over four hundred per cent.'

'It was sold again in 1984.' She glanced at her notes. 'For £16,428.'

'Nearly doubled in four years. Who sold it?'

'Christie's New York.'

'*New York?* That means the bloody thing's almost certainly in America. Anything after that? Nearer to now?'

'Nothing, Tim.'

'Damn! What does it look like, I wonder?' I gestured at her. 'Try the RA catalogues in bound copies over there. Mr Goodston said it was the 1923 winner. Try that year and 1924; I think that 1924 is the year.'

She nipped back to the shelves and looked, almost excitedly. After a hurried flip through and a check on the index at the back of each year, disappointment flooded her face. 'They've only illustrated his portraits. Of boring people. No Sergeant Murphy here at all.'

'Pity.' I had a quick think. 'I really want to know what it looked like. It's not illustrated in Bruce Arnold's book on Orpen 'cos I've checked at home. Try the *Dictionary of Equestrian Artists*, in those lower shelves. See what it says under Orpen. If anything.'

She knelt to the lower shelves and pulled out the dictionary, leafing through its alphabetical order quickly.

This time her face beamed.

'Look! It's here! It's an awfully small picture, but it's here!'

She put the heavy book on my desk, open at the Orpen entry. I took up a magnifying glass and stared at a small black and white illustration of two smartly-dressed men, one capped, one trilbyed, clad in riding breeches of almost military cut with polished long boots, staring at a jockey on a brown horse, which occupied most of the right-centre of the painting. In the landscaped background, a distant race of perhaps ten horses was passing a finishing post beneath rolling countryside. To the right foreground a country boy was leaning against a tree. Something about him reminded me of Orpen himself, but the print was too small to be sure.

'"Sergeant Murphy and Things",' I murmured.

'There was even a portrait of Sir Alfred Munnings by Orpen.' Penny's voice was still a bit excited. 'A pencil sketch. Sold for £650 in 1985, according to the *Index*.'

The brown horse had a semi-white forefoot and the back legs had two white socks up to the ankles. The two proprietorial men looked at it proudly. It was still so clear in my mind that it was unmistakable.

It was the right-hand horse in the oil sketch in Ted Murphy's flat.

'Damn it!' I said out loud. 'Damn it, damn it, damn it! Sergeant bloody Murphy. Munnings, too. Now *that's* a connection.'

The office door opened and a blond head came round.

'Time for lunch.' Jeremy White's voice was jovial. 'Doesn't anyone ever get hungry around here?'

CHAPTER 16

'These people do a very good Griotte Chambertin,' Jeremy said, reflectively, rolling the rich red Burgundy round in his glass. 'One gets a little sleepy with claret at lunch time and the Beaujolais are perhaps a bit light for special occasions, but a good Côte de Nuits fills the bill perfectly. What was the saying? – I can't think who it was – "I forget the name of the place, I forget the name of the girl, but the wine was Chambertin." Who was that?'

'Hilaire Belloc, I think, Jeremy.'

'Ah, Belloc. Yes of course. What a memory you have, Tim.'

'Special occasion? Far be it for me to discourage the Burgundy, but is this a special occasion?'

'Of course it is! Of course it is! We lunch so infrequently nowadays, Tim. In Park Lane days it was a regular occurrence. A regular occurrence. Ah, what happy times those were. The City is a melancholy spectacle by comparison. No one lunches, seriously lunches, I mean, any more. Long faces at Lloyds, sadness at the Stock Exchange, spurious fraud accusations creeping down every corridor. Economic turmoil worldwide.' He shook his head gloomily as the waiter refilled his glass with the expensive fluid. 'No leadership. No forward thinking. Still' – he took a sip and cheered a little – 'we must not allow ourselves to become despondent. The bright side first; best foot forward. We are celebrating, however mutedly, a major acquisition. It is not every day, Tim, that we can pull off a coup like the Crockingham Collection.' He peered at me. 'I do hope that you are not still a contra rather than a pro? Recent, er, recent, um, *events* have not further entrenched your opposition?'

'The events, as you so euphemistically call them, have not altered my opinion, no. The Collection contains far too much journeyman stuff for my liking. On the other hand, I still rather like the Munnings, despite what Sue says.'

'Sue says? Is she frightfully opposed?'

'I'm afraid horses do not inspire her, Jeremy, and Munnings positively switches her *off*.'

'Oh dear. All the more credit to you, Tim, dear boy, for being so positive about that aspect of the Collection.'

'The Carberrys' paintings by Munnings are not half bad. They're not like his horse and rider portraits, which bore me to death. I suppose he had to earn a living somehow. He had a wife to keep in horses and other expenses, although to her credit she always said that those wealthy potboilers were not up to much. She actually said, apparently, that he was never so good a painter after he married her because he had to take too commercial a view of his painting. Didn't have time to do the stuff he really liked.'

'Oh. Well, that was, as you say, to her credit.'

I smiled. 'Talking of credit, Jeremy, who actually owns the Crockingham Collection?'

His head reared up sharply. 'Owns. Who owns? Sir Andrew Carberry, of course.'

'Does he? In his personal capacity?'

'Oh.' Comprehension dawned on his face. 'I see what you're driving at. No, it's not quite like that. The Collection is owned by a holding company. Part of his rather complex financial arrangements. When we purchase the Collection we will either buy the shares of the company and thus own the Collection which comprises its assets, or the company will sell us the Collection outright.'

'Well, which is it to be?'

Jeremy waved a vague butter knife. 'Geoffrey is sorting all that out. Making the best tax and legal provisions. Usual sort of thing.'

'So – if I've got this straight – we will either buy up a company which owns the Collection, or we will buy the Collection off that company. Not from Sir Andrew himself.'

'Exactly, Tim.'

'And the Collection, that is to say what the Collection comprises, will be defined by whatever is on the books of the company we buy?'

'Of course.' His brow furrowed a little. 'What exactly are you driving at?'

'Oh, nothing. Just getting it all quite clear in my mind, that's

116

all. I imagine the company will prove its title to the Collection in some proper way? It's not how we've acquired paintings before, you see.'

'I realize that. But Sir Andrew had his own good reasons for putting the Collection into a corporate ownership, of course. There were tax matters to consider. As for title, I'm sure there will be absolutely clear documentation on that score.'

'Of course,' I responded drily. 'Although he seems to have taken a rather liberal view of what is his and what should be corporate in the past.'

'Tim, really. You mustn't repeat old rumours and vague criticisms of that sort, you know. It won't do at all. That was all cleared up long ago. Anyway, if he created all those assets, he understandably views them as his, er, his –'

'Possessions?'

'Of course not. Not necessarily. More his, um, sphere of influence, you might say.'

'Ah. Dictators tend to use that phrase when invading adjacent territory. Tell me, Jeremy: why did he resign his seat as an MP?'

Jeremy brought his blond eyebrows together in a frown. 'Tim, I really don't think there's anything to be gained by exploring this line of country. You have a distressing tendency to see everything in, how shall I put it, criminal terms. Such is not the case this time.'

'I'm delighted to hear it. But why?'

A nettled look came to his face. 'There were, apparently, some auditors' qualifications to the accounts of one, or it may have been more than one, of his companies.'

'His companies? Publicly-quoted companies, were they?'

'Well, yes, they were, but for heaven's sake stop barking up that particular tree. You know what auditors are like. They so often take a tedious attitude to quite straightforward transactions. It was all perfectly satisfactorily explained and cleared up afterwards. While the whole thing was being given quite unnecessary publicity by the gutter press, however, he felt it would remove any embarrassment to the then prime minister to stand down; there was an election at just about that time and he gracefully withdrew.' Jeremy picked up his glass and took another appreciative sip from it. 'I always thought it was very loyal of him to do that. Self-sacrificing, in fact. He was

117

rather keen on the idea of a political career for a time and it was a blow to him.'

'I see.'

'Do you? I wonder if you do, you know. There's an element of scurrilous scepticism about you these days, Tim, which seems to be getting more pronounced with time rather than diminishing.' He sighed heavily. 'It's a sign of the times, of course.'

'Now you're talking like a seventy-year-old, Jeremy, instead of a man in his prime. Scepticism is an Anglo-Saxon characteristic, like truculence, humour and pugnacity. It's very healthy.'

'Hmm.' It was almost a snort, but he smiled after it. Jeremy likes to think of himself as being in his prime. 'You may be right. But we have to tread carefully where Sir Andrew is concerned. Very carefully. He is important to us. And he's suffered a tragic blow. A tragic blow.' He swirled the wine round in his glass. 'Richard and I will, of course, be going to the funeral when it takes place. I gather that the police will allow the, um, the body to be collected for burial shortly. They're quite satisfied about the cause of death. She was unconscious when the body entered the water. Quite horrifying, really. One wonders who could have done such a terrible thing. The ex-husband, perhaps.'

'The Cambridge police will be doing all the necessary there, Jeremy.'

'Indeed. Indeed.' He shot me a sharp look. 'There is no cause for your – for your discovery of the body – very distressing for you, of course – to warrant further – further –'

'Intervention?'

'Precisely, Tim! Precisely! Couldn't have put it better myself. Although I must say I, um, I understand Sir Andrew's, um, concern that you should have been present at her cottage at the time.'

'Ah.' We were coming to the purpose of the lunch. 'Sir Andrew has called you to express his *concern*, has he?'

'Well – actually – yes, he has. He seemed to think that an employee of the bank should, er, should observe very scrupulous procedure when dealing, er, with the family of a client such as himself and, in particular, with, with –'

'Attractive female members of the family in solitary and compromising circumstances?'

He swallowed without apparently having anything in his

throat to swallow. 'You put it, as usual, in your own customary manner. But I think that is what he meant, yes.'

'You think? If I know Sir Andrew, he put it to you in terms which left you in no doubt.' I grinned at him. 'I'm grateful to you, Jeremy, for being so characteristically tactful. Don't think I don't appreciate the trouble I may have caused you.'

'Oh, Tim! My dear fellow! We have been friends long enough, surely, for us to be able to be absolutely frank with one another? Have you no idea why that woman lured you up to Fen Ditton – Fen Ditton of all places; one remembers glorious picnics on that long grassy bank there in one's youth – on your own? To tell you what? For what purpose?'

'Sorry, Jeremy. I really haven't. But she certainly didn't want anyone else to know. Since we had only met the day before about the Art Fund and the Collection, I assumed at first it would be something to do with that. Then I saw that Ted Murphy had posted his card to me from Cambridge. It seemed too much of a coincidence. God, I've been through all this *ad infinitum* with the police. I've even – this very morning – been through the most horrendous set of photos in Ted Murphy's snap album to see if there could be a connection. There isn't. Not from that evidence, anyway. So I don't know.'

'Oh dear. Well, Sir Andrew was not best pleased. He thought it would give the newspapers grounds for unsavoury speculation. I had to make myself very clear to him about that, though. I told him I had no doubt that you, as a director of the Fund, would doubtless behave at all times with scrupulous propriety and decorum.'

I chuckled, thinking of Jeremy's recent fulminations on the rugby club dinner. 'Thank you, Jeremy. What did he say to that?'

Jeremy frowned. 'He said he was not so sure.'

'Oh? What did he mean?'

'I think, you know, Tim, that you sometimes forget that your reputation is more widespread than you think. There has been, in the past, some press coverage of cases in which you have featured somewhat sensationally. Sir Andrew, I think, was referring implicitly to those.'

'Really? I had no idea that I was that famous. Perhaps that's why he called me a snoop.'

'A snoop?' Jeremy bridled. 'A snoop? Did he say that?'

'He did. And he sent me to the tradesman's entrance when I went to Crockingham. But that's just his style; I didn't know he knew who I was in the other sense, then.'

'Oh, I think you can be sure he does his research. He didn't make his millions in ignorance.'

'Or lose them again in it?'

'Ha! Lloyds has caught a lot of people napping, Tim. The excess market was a roller coaster. Thank God none of us at the bank got caught. Gambling of that sort was never our thing. But it's caught the Carberrys hard. Very hard.'

'Well,' I took a swallow from my own glass, 'they've got a stay of execution with the Fund's acquisition. It remains to be seen whether they can keep hold of the rest.'

'It does indeed.' Jeremy was starting to look brighter. 'But let us not dwell upon the more depressing things, Tim. I'm so glad that we've had this very pleasant lunch together. Cleared the air, so to speak. You and I have been through far too much together to let such matters cloud our days. In due course the tragic circumstances will be settled by the police. The Fund will continue to prosper. We mustn't let things get out of proportion. We both have many other concerns to occupy us. Uncle Richard is going to need your help in France again, soon. There is Brazil to think about. I do hope these matters have not taken your eye off the ball, so to speak?'

'No, no.' He and Sergeant Will Cook had an expression in common, if little else. 'I will be replying to Brazil this afternoon.'

'Oh, good. Good. I wouldn't like to think that the Fund was bulking too large in our concerns.'

'Not at all, Jeremy. I have many other matters on my plate just now.'

Including, I didn't tell him, the reading of three volumes of autobiography and one of biography, as quickly as I bloody well – Munnings's imprecations must be infectious – could.

CHAPTER 17

Ghosts, Mr Goodston had said, in his shop. It looked as though I had been visited by ghosts.

I stood at the long living room window, staring out at the morning shine of plane trees reflected on the roofs of cars in Onslow Gardens. I was considering how many ghosts one man's autobiography could conjure up within the rambling, discursive, but vivid pages of memories put together by someone who was forty when the First World War ended. Someone in whose mind, like Bertrand Russell's, the England of pre-1914 always lingered as a lost Arcadia, whether it was or not. People forget how bloody awful this country must have been in 1950, when Munnings was writing his memoirs. Rationing and small-minded taxation; little meat and bloody small beer. Council estates and bungalow-rash covering what were once lush fields bordered by hedgerow oaks grown in the slow-moving days of full, sluggish rivers posted with polled willows. It must have been easy to hate what you saw.

You did not have to have been a gilded Edwardian aristocrat to recall, in late Victorian and Edwardian England, a rich para-dise of rumbustious countrymen bred on beef and beer, cursing genially at horses whilst entranced by mysterious, colourfully-clothed women. A poster-printer's apprentice could do that. You did not have to be a landowner to remember 1904 as the year of Cockburn's port, any more than you had to be an indulged young idler to enjoy the Bohemian Paris of Julian's *atelier* before the motor car destroyed the ambience of the Boul-evard St Germain. It was not considered naïve, then, to stumble upon the great battle paintings of Morot and de Neuville, and cherish them as magnificent achievements. That was before the Luxembourg Galleries started to fill with modern 'distorted drolleries' needing an expensive art education to understand them. Munnings experienced all of these things on an expenditure of shillings, not pounds.

Ghosts were certainly in my mind; the ghost of Reuben Levine of Norwich, dealer in old silver and rare books, who sold Munnings his fine copy of Stubbs's *Anatomy of the Horse*, the one Mr Goodston eventually saw, full size and original edition, for fifty shillings.

The ghost of a painter called J. Hobart, whose depiction of a grey horse called Orinoco, the property of William Green Munnings of Stoke-by-Nayland in 1840, was seen every morning at prayers by the grandchild A. J. Munnings in the 1880s. Grey horses were always his delight and he thought often of horse and heifer portraitists like Hobart and their lives as a sort of earlier model of his own. This then, must be the horse-painting ancestor of whom the curator at Crockingham had spoken.

Ghosts like another grey, a tram-horse belonging to local Mendham farmer Ben Cook, painted amongst the buttercups; the only accepted painting, for Munnings, one year at the Royal Academy. That horse had come to rural Mendham from the London General Omnibus Company and had worked the No. 14 route from Putney to Liverpool Street, where Munnings would arrive by train. The Putney bus, Munnings said, was an all-white horse route, and the greys were bred in Ireland for the purpose.

Ghosts; the Putney bus, when I lived in the Fulham Road not so far from Ted Murphy, and Jeremy and I worked in Park Lane, was the one I used to walk up the Little Boltons to catch in the Old Brompton Road just west of Peter Blackwell's shop at the Drayton Gardens crossroads. My stroll took me past the end of South Bolton Gardens, where Orpen had his studio and drank himself to death. Whenever I think of Orpen I always think of fair Yvonne Aubicq and then of Marianne Gray, the American lady who looked like her, especially with no clothes on, who caused such violent events while Sue was away in Australia and Nobby had to save my life.

It was in South Bolton Gardens, near the Putney bus route, where Orpen, the most famous and the richest portrait painter of his day, was said to make his wealthy clients queue outside in their Rolls Royces while they waited their turn to be painted. What Munnings was to horses, Orpen was to people. Whenever I see Orpen's painting of Yvonne sitting nude on a bed in the morning sunlight, reading a letter with her knees drawn up, in a relaxed pose and totally absorbed, with her coffee untouched beside her, I think of Marianne.

Had Ted Murphy guessed at that particular ghost of mine when we talked of Orpen? With Irish intuition he might have detected something of the feelings that Orpen associations raise in me. That card was cleverly sent; he must have known that once it reached me I would never rest until its mystery was resolved.

Orpen's presence flits through the memories in Munnings's volumes: serious at a chateau in France during the war, whimsical at the Arts Club in Dover Street, painting the company at the Café Royal or the chef at the Hotel Meurice, dining at Wyndham's, bibulous in Chelsea. But Orpen is always the Royal Academician, exhibiting, professional, expensive and, in that one famous case, a peer of Munnings on his own ground. Until the weakness which Munnings shared with him finally destroyed his health, you feel that his celebrated shadow slips in and out of the pages, a luminous wisp for Munnings to try and rival.

Then there was another, even less substantial ghost: the ghost of Tissot, who lightly haunts the pages of Munnings's memories, not only in the huge painting he lent to the Dover Street Arts Club and which he called '*Le Danseuse de Cord*', destroyed by a bomb which hit the Club in the Second World War. That would be the painting Christopher Wood and James Wentworth, in their books on Tissot, call '*L'Acrobate*' – 'The Tight-Rope Dancer' – and say the whereabouts is unknown even though Munnings's description of it is dead accurate. That painting will never again be seen by human eye.

Tissot's most famous masterpiece, on the other hand, no spectre at all, had come to the eyes of both Sue and me most graphically once –

'Tim?' Sue had come out of the bedroom wrapped in a gown, tousled but wide-eyed, to stare at me. 'Have you been up all night?'

Manet, Degas, and Tissot; Munnings admired all three, perhaps knowing or sensing the bonds between them.

'Tim?' Her voice was harassed.

'Sorry. I was miles away. Yes, most of it. I've been reading.'

'All night?'

'Nearly. Sue, do you remember when we went down into the

basement of the Tate to look at Tissot's "The Ball on Shipboard" together?'

'Of course I do. Tim, it'll do your health no good –'

'That painting was bought for the Tate by the Chantrey Bequest.'

'I know that. Tim –'

'Guess who they bought it from?'

She blinked. 'I've no idea.'

'Munnings.'

'*Munnings?*' The blink was much more pronounced this time, preceding a white flash of the eyes, which stared at me in disbelief.

'Yes, Munnings. He puts it in his book quite casually. Lord Sandwich and J. B. Manson came to his studio to buy it in 1937 or so, for six hundred pounds. While they were there they saw Munnings's "Return from Ascot", so they bought that, too. That was the one Sir John Rothenstein never hung up, presumably to pay Munnings back for nasty remarks.'

'But Munnings owned "The Ball on Shipboard"?'

'Yes.'

She shivered slightly and drew the gown closer about her. 'How very sinister. Where did he get it from?'

'He doesn't say. Tissots often sold for forty pounds or so before 1914. And even after the war. Munnings collected all sorts of things. It's not sinister, it's just a ghostly coincidence.'

'Ghostly? I think that it's very sinister. You'd better have some breakfast.'

She bustled into the kitchenette, thus showing that she was not calm. Sue is not domestically inclined and does not normally get breakfast. In fact, a kitchenette-presence means, nearly always, emotional agitation. This time my information meant that she felt more than a little involved. When I was researching Tissot before an earlier purchase for the Fund, Sue took me down the basement of the Tate to look at 'The Ball on Shipboard', because I thought it had connotations involving Moreton Frewen and other matters. It was part of our history. To find that Munnings had owned the painting – not currently on display and therefore immured in the Tate's subterranean store – struck a solemn and, I had to agree, slightly spooky chord. Reading and researching occasionally does that to you. In a mind-occupying jumble of facts and dates and figures, clear resonances from other, overlapping and past associations can have an over-emphasized impact. Sue's reaction wasn't surprising.

Her voice came out over the clatter of a poaching pan.

'What else have you discovered?'

'What else? What else?' I turned away from the window. 'Well, it's all in those books. Illustrated, for instance, on page 241, volume two, in black and white: "Sergeant Murphy and The Drifter". A painting of two horses, very relaxed, in a paddock. Munnings says he never did anything better. He'd already painted the trainer, George Blackwell, holding Sergeant Murphy in an official version for the owner, Mr Sandford, but on a quiet day at Snailwell –that's just north of Newmarket – in front of a clunch wall, he painted the two horses together with the Saxon church tower in the background. A sort of pleasure exercise. But it's the finished version of the oil sketch in Ted Murphy's living room. Stopped me short in my reading. No doubt of it.'

She came out of the kitchenette, face closing with thought and concern. 'Where is it now?'

'No idea. A dealer bought it and sold it to Sandford, who owned both horses. Ted's version must be one of the artist's working, preparatory things. Munnings often did watercolours or smaller versions of paintings, things like Ted's, before launching into a finished work.'

'What was "The Drifter"?'

'Finished second in the 1922 National. Another brown horse.'

'Horses,' she muttered. 'All those horses.'

'Orpen and Munnings painted the same horse. Around 1923, when Sergeant Murphy won the National. The two well-breeched men in Orpen's version must be Sandford and Blackwell. Orpen's was exhibited in 1924 at the Royal Academy and that's when Munnings was a bit piqued to hear some people thought Orpen had done a better horse than the one Munnings exhibited. The two artists had met before, of course, because they stayed at the same château when they were war artists in 1918 and they both painted the Canadians together. Munnings pinched Orpen's brushes. They knew each other quite well afterwards, too; drank at the same clubs, that sort of thing.'

'But Ted Murphy sent you a card with an Orpen message,

not a Munnings. He surely didn't mean to sell you the painting in his living room, did he?'

'I don't know. There's another thing. Murphy's real name – his name at birth – was Pulham. Pulham turns out to be a village not far from Mendham, but over on the Norfolk side. Munnings mentions people who lived at Pulham Hall. I mean, Pulham is not an uncommon name – there was a Pulham at school with me – but it's the Norfolk thing, you see. Orpen's family origin was Norfolk, too. There was something that had got Ted Murphy all excited, but what exactly it was makes my head spin. I can't work it out; too many bits and pieces, not fitting together.'

'I think you should forget about it. I know you won't, but that's my advice.' Sue's voice was determined. 'It'll do no good and whatever it was is probably best forgotten. It'll be all to do with those women in the photographs. You said that Mr Goodston said *cherchez la femme*. Well, I'm sure he's right.'

'And Liz – Elizabeth Dennison? What about her murder?'

'That'll be something like the same thing. You can't – '

The telephone rang, interrupting her and making her scowl. I picked up the receiver as she went back to the poaching pan, noting steam issuing from somewhere.

'Tim?'

The voice was calm, oldish, cultured. Sir Richard White always sounds unruffled.

'Good morning, Richard.' I tried to sound the same.

'Good morning. Rather more advanced here than with you. I'm at the office at Maucourt's. I'm sorry to disturb you at home but I'm glad I've caught you before you went out.' His allusion to the hour's time difference between London and Paris was slightly tongue in cheek; it being still only seven-thirty in London, he must have got to his office pretty early. 'I need to know if you are fully occupied on Friday?'

'Friday? Next Friday? No, I don't think so.'

'Oh, good. I'll tell Jeremy, then. You see, I have to go to Lyon for a most important meeting. I'll convey my regrets to Sir Andrew and confirm that I've asked you to take my place.'

'Place. What place?'

'At the funeral. Elizabeth Dennison's funeral. You weren't to know, but I've just heard it's to be on Friday. Normally, I would have gone with Jeremy to pay the bank's respects, et cetera, but this meeting is a Ministry of Finance matter and you know

126

what the French are like about that sort of thing. I simply have to be there. I'm sure it's most appropriate that you take my place in view of the Fund's acquisition and so on. And of your own – what – extraordinary involvement, so to speak.'

'Er, well, in that respect, Richard, I should tell you that Sir Andrew isn't altogether enamoured – I mean, I might be just a little *de trop*, you might say, in view of some remarks he's made to Jeremy about my, um, my being on the scene.'

'Oh, I know.' The voice was still unruffled, urbane, cultured. 'I know all about that, Tim.'

'You do?'

'Oh, yes. I got the message quite clearly. That's why I want you to go.'

'What?'

'I'm sure I can rely on your judgement, Tim.'

'Richard?'

'And your sense of decorum.'

'Eh?'

'I'll tell Jeremy.'

'But –'

He'd already put his phone down; I was left standing, holding my receiver.

Sue came into the room with a plate of toast and poached eggs. 'Who was that?'

'Sir Richard White. From Paris. He wants me to go to the funeral.'

'Funeral? What funeral?'

'Elizabeth Dennison's. At Crockingham.'

'Elizabeth Dennison's?' She bridled visibly. 'What on earth for?'

'Business, I imagine. He says he can't make it himself. So I'm to go in his place.' I smiled and sat down at the table as she put the eggs in front of me. 'It's just a matter of business, Sue. Just business.' I widened my smile condescendingly. 'You know how it is. No need for you to worry your pretty little –'

She moved quickly but I just managed to grab her right arm in time.

Otherwise the poached eggs would have been spread all over her husband.

CHAPTER 18

'Things have perked up quite a lot,' Sergeant Will Cook said with satisfaction, eyeing his bottled Pale Ale complacently. 'Quite a lot, I'm glad to say. We've got Banks back in irons again. Caught him hiding over a betting shop in the Seven Sisters area. With two chums who correspond to the van hold-up men. Tip-off from a well-wisher, so to speak.'

'Oh, good. Nobby must be pleased.' I nodded approvingly as I sipped my bitter. We were back, at Cook's telephoned request, to the pub in the Fulham Road. Outside, frustrated traffic ground past the congested pavements of the shop-soiled thoroughfare, providing a sort of thunderous, battle-background noise to the mahogany-lined, flock-papered and faded gloom of the saloon bar. 'Like Eugene Aram, is he?'

'Sorry?'

' "Between stern-faced men, with gyves upon his wrists? That sort of thing?" '

'Oh.' Cook still looked mystified. His reading matter obviously didn't include Hood, or even Bertie Wooster's variations of Hood. 'We don't go in for gyves much, but I'm sure he's shut up safe and sound, if that's what you mean. Out of reach of his pals and going through rather intense questioning, just now.'

'I'm sure he is.' I gave Cook a quizzical glance. 'Thumbscrews? Red-hot needles under the fingernails? Horse-size injections of mind-releasing drugs? What do you use nowadays?'

Cook frowned disapprovingly. 'That's not funny, you know. Everything has to be by the book. Even a nasty piece of work like Banks'll have all the protection the law allows him, I'm sorry to say.'

'Oh. Bit of a handicap for you, that. I must admit that I haven't much sympathy for him. Still haven't got my car back yet.'

'Mmm.' Cook considered his Pale Ale again thoughtfully. 'Well. These things take time. It does mean we can get on with the Murphy case uninterrupted, though – that's the main thing.'

'Good.'

'Which is why I asked you if we could have another chat down here today.'

'Feel free. Here I am.'

'You haven't had any more thoughts?'

'Thoughts? Oh, about the meaning of Ted's message and so on. No, I can't say that I have. I rack my brains but I'm just churning over the same old ground. What about you? Have you found any more of the ladies of the album? Or rather albums?'

He nodded. 'We've identified one or two more, yes. Through asking around locally.' He glanced up from his beer as though to conjure up images right there in the saloon bar. 'And we've eliminated them from our inquiries. They were either far away or their current gentlemen friends and spouses were far enough away to be certain they couldn't be involved.' He sighed. 'It's a long, tedious process. From the papers in his desk, we've found a lawyer that Murphy used from time to time and, through him, a will. It benefits a male cousin in Ireland called Pulham. He's in the clear, too – he was fishing near Cork with friends at the time of the murder – so if there was a motive there, it doesn't signify. The stock in Murphy's shop will mostly go to paying off a bank loan on the business anyway, so the cousin won't get a lot. But there'll be something. We don't think Murphy was blackmailing anyone. At least there are no lush bank statements or savings accounts full of money, or unaccountable payments that would indicate that sort of thing. And the, er, participants in his little albums we've found so far have said there was nothing like that. In fact, they were pretty shocked to be told they had been, er, recorded for posterity in that way. First time they'd heard of it.'

'So you think the photos were just for his own amusement?'

'It looks like it.'

'What about his purchase ledger? Is there a chance he might have logged the purchase of the Orpen painting in it? He might have taken a flyer on buying it, although I don't think he had that sort of money, recently. More likely he would have been selling it for someone. Running it, as they say in the trade.'

'Ah. That's why I asked you here. Maybe if you look at his books you'll identify something that'll lead us back to it. It's only a chance, but it's worth trying.'

'Of course. Only too glad to help. I'd be interested to know where he bought that oil of "Sergeant Murphy and The Drifter" in the living room, too. The Munnings. If he's recorded it. That might give us a clue. Then there's his petrol receipts. Any leads there?'

'London, Cambridge.' Cook began to tick off places on his fingers. 'Newmarket, Membury – that's the M4 service area – London again. That covers the last two weeks.'

'So that holds no surprises, except Membury, which could be a trip to anywhere out west including, say, Cheltenham Races. OK: I'll come and look at the purchase ledger and receipts.'

'Fine. Well, we'll just wait for DCI Roberts to arrive and then we'll go and open up.'

'Nobby? Here? You mean he's joining us now?'

Cook nodded solidly. 'Oh, yes. He was very specific about that. We're to wait until he arrives.'

This took me a bit aback. 'I'm amazed. Surely he'll be too busy with Banks to get here today?'

'Oh, no. There's plenty to keep Banks from nodding off, let me tell you. There's relays of them wanting to talk to Banks. If you hold up a police van at gunpoint and release a dangerous criminal, it's surprising how garrulous we can be.'

'I'm sure. That's why I'm impressed with his zeal for the Fulham Road.'

'DCI Roberts is very keen to get this and the Cambridge murder cleared up, I can tell you. He's pressing Goodall up in Cambridge pretty hard.'

'That sounds like my Nobby. He –'

I was interrupted. The door to the street opened and Nobby himself came striding in, all gingery action and alertness, like an Airedale after a dustman.

I waved him towards us. 'Hello, Nobby. This is a pleasant surprise. Let me get you a bitter?'

'Thanks. A half will be enough.' He gave me a quick scrutiny and turned to Cook. 'How's it going, Will?'

'Pretty steady. Found one or two more. No real breakthrough yet.'

The rest of the answer was lost in the heavy rumble of a passing pantechnicon which deafened me as I went to the bar. The pub was uncomfortably close to the road. I got back with

Nobby's glass in hand to find him seated behind the table, next to Cook, regarding me brightly.

'I gather Will has told you about our recapture of Banks?'

'Oh, yes. Congratulations all round, I suppose?'

'Should never have lost him in the first place.' He took the glass with an affable nod. 'Pretty slipshod, they were, with that van. Anyway, it's all over now. Until the next time. Cheers!'

'Cheers!' I regarded him cautiously. Something about his manner was unsettling me. At work, Nobby is rarely affable, especially with me. He affects a tough, suspicious mien, particularly in front of subordinates. It's possibly my fault because I can't help joshing him and he's usually on the defensive. Yet today he seemed very cheerful, even breezy. It must be this recapture of Banks, I thought, that's putting him into such an overtly good mood.

'I must say, I'm impressed,' I said, 'to see you down here, Nobby. Thought you'd be far too busy for this.'

'Ah, no.' He shook his head emphatically. 'Got my priorities right this time.'

'Oh?'

'Yes.' He held up his glass and looked at the bit of froth on top of the beer with interest. 'Quite an interview I had with Banks, though. Quite an interview. Exhaustive, you might say.'

'I'm sure.'

'Are you? Yes, I expect you are.' He nodded thoughtfully. 'There's an aspect of it which I thought might interest you, actually.'

'Me? What?'

Nobby smiled blandly. I didn't like it at all. Pleasant perspectives and interesting aspects are not part of Nobby's working attitude to me.

Then he spoke, using a sort of reportage style which was ominous.

'As a result of an extensive interview with Banks – in which I had a more than personal interest, as you might imagine – we have established, without the shadow of any doubt – I assure you the inquiries were extremely intense – that neither Banks nor his associates could possibly have been in or near Cambridge on the day you found the body of Elizabeth Dennison.'

I frowned. 'Eh?'

'Not a hope. And, if they could not have been in Cambridge,

they could not have placed a bomb under your car.' He smiled, cat-like now, drawing my undivided attention. 'And, therefore, could not – a fact which they indignantly aver in the strongest possible terms, but then they would, wouldn't they; it's the evidence that counts – have been aiming to end my existence. Nothing personal at all, Banks claims, in his approach to me.'

'Hang on, Nobby, hang on –'

But he was remorseless.

'And therefore, if they were not responsible, then it is extremely unlikely, given the circumstances and the vehicle in question, that I was the target of the bomb that was placed under it.' He smiled again and sipped a little beer so that the froth just deposited a gentle, thin, elderly moustache of foam on to his freckled upper lip as his eyes held mine in a direct, piercing stare. 'Which leads one to another, much more logical conclusion.'

He licked the froth away with a pink, healthy tongue and cocked his head to one side as he still held my now near-paralysed gaze of horror with his own genial expression.

'You must admit that it wouldn't be the first time, would it, Tim?'

CHAPTER 19

In the evening I took Sue out to dinner at a little place in the Old Brompton Road. I needed help.

I waited until we had eaten our meal, washed down with a bottle of Fleurie, and then I told her just exactly how everything stood, exactly what had happened, and when.

She asked for a brandy with her coffee.

'I haven't told anyone else about this,' I said. I ordered a brandy for myself, too.

'Not even Jeremy?'

'Especially not Jeremy. I'll have to tell him tomorrow, but I couldn't face it today.'

'But you'll have to tell him, all the same. With the Elizabeth Dennison aspect, this could be part of the Crockingham situation, not just Ted Murphy.'

I nodded. The impact of the threat was still sinking in. Had the bomb under my Jaguar gone off with me and Nobby inside the car, the world would have assumed that Nobby was the intended victim. It would have taken months to sort out the truth. I wondered whether the assassin knew that or whether Nobby's presence was purely incidental, a sort of additional bonus which would have complicated things in the assassin's favour. Nobby himself had now become infuriatingly patronizing towards me, condescendingly pointing out that he, after all, was not in any way to blame for the car bomb incident and that this was yet another in a long series of unpleasant episodes which he, Nobby, had had to endure due to my irresponsible behaviour. And so on and so on *ad nauseam* until I had to snap at him to stop pi-jawing like a bloody old woman and get his dilatory forces to pull their combined fingers out for a change. That didn't please him at all, but since it was now my life on the line, I wasn't too concerned about the niceties of his feelings in front of Sergeant Will Cook.

133

We had proceeded to Ted Murphy's flat in ill humour, battling our way down a crowded Fulham Road in irritable convoy. The shop looked even dustier and more unsuccessful than it had before, with the terrible, badly-hung splashy watercolour of shire horses over the desk ploughing their brown field and reflecting the front windows as I headed for the account books. Nobby and Will Cook decided to give the place another thorough search as I scanned Ted Murphy's records. I must say they were thorough; they looked into everything that opened or shut and they even looked behind the paintings on the walls. I had to move over for Cook to shift the splashy watercolour in its big Victorian frame, but there was nothing behind it but darker plaster than the surrounding material. They went through the stacks on the floor; they tapped floorboards while they were doing it; they opened every single drawer, looked inside lampshades, peered into the longcase clock, took its hood off and gaped at the works, upended vases, scowled into a specimen cabinet, delved with disgust into a mouldy Davenport whose lid was stuck down with chewing gum. Nothing came of it.

The books told me nothing either. They were reasonably well kept, but used those admirably cryptic descriptions of pieces which enable dealers to ensure their transferability. A cupboard or a bureau or a chest of drawers described in simple terms may be bought and sold within the books regardless of the real transactions any of those pieces or others of similar description may have generated. There is no point in being too specific merely to benefit a tax inspector or, more particularly, the severe operation of Value Added Tax by the zealous Gestapo of the Customs and Excise Department. Some of the paintings had to be quite accurately specified, of course, and in those cases the names of the artists were clearly written into the books. Some, however, were not. The splashy watercolour behind me was merely noted as a 'Ploughing Scene' and there was a 'Horse in Paddock' bought and sold for prices which could not have been anywhere near those of the Munnings upstairs. Of a Munnings or an Orpen there was no mention.

We went upstairs, where Nobby and Will Cook proceeded to repeat their efforts of the shop and I gazed for a bit at the 'Sergeant Murphy and The Drifter' sketch before taking it gently off the wall and looking at the back.

It was framed in quite a heavy moulding for a relatively small canvas – about twenty-four inches by thirty – and was fairly dusty. The stretcher of the canvas had a couple of exhibition labels stuck to it, but they were faded numbers without explanation.

Much more important, there was a piece of lined writing paper folded and wedged between canvas and stretcher at the bottom edge. I took it out carefully, put the painting down, and opened the paper up on the table nearby. There was writing on it, in ink, which I did not recognize as Ted's own.

'Sergeant Murphy and The Drifter' it said. *A. J. Munnings, PRA. Painted at Snailwell, 1924.*

That was all.

I knew that, I wanted to shout at it. I found that out for myself. Damn it, I knew that already. So, obviously, did Ted.

The only way Ted would know that would be if the vendor told him, or someone like Mr Goodston told him, or if he owned a copy of Munnings's autobiography, the full three volumes, not the abbreviated version. There was nothing in the Orpen biography about it, nor a picture of Orpen's own painting. Ted was an Orpen fan, not a Munnings fan. I scanned his bookcase quickly and then went downstairs to search the one he had behind his desk there. No copy of the Munnings autobiography was to be seen.

So someone told him. Most likely the owner of the painting, the one who had sold it to Ted. If Ted had actually bought it outright and was not running it for someone. And every time I thought of horse paintings I thought of Crockingham and Ted being at Newmarket and Elizabeth Dennison's body in the reeds at the river bank.

But the Crockingham catalogue had no painting of 'Sergeant Murphy and The Drifter' in it. I checked when I got back to the bank. So it couldn't have come from Crockingham.

I was back where I started. Yet I had knowledge, or was assumed to have knowledge, which someone thought so dangerous that they were willing to blow me sky-high to prevent it getting out. Nobby promised to have someone keep a regular eye on the flat so that Sue wouldn't be endangered and asked me to advise Will Cook of all my movements so that they could, if they thought it advisable, provide protection. Goodall, for instance, was going to be at the Crockingham funeral. But full-time personal protection was ruled out.

'You're not Salman Rushdie,' was what Nobby said, unkindly. 'We can't afford full-time resources. Anyway, in view of your past record and your own actions, the taxpayer can expect you to look after yourself most of the time.'

'Thanks very much.'

'And if anything – I really mean anything – happens or occurs to you in thinking things over, you tell us. Right?'

'Right.'

'We'll be in touch. Soon.'

'How reassuring.'

We parted on reasonable terms, Nobby still elated to have regained his moral ascendancy and me too preoccupied to waste time urging him to get a move on before someone succeeded in doing me in. I went back to work, to check up on a few things and to clear my desk before the day of the funeral.

I avoided Jeremy.

Sue was looking at me across the dinner table with the look she gets when I find myself in these situations. A sort of quizzical and exasperated look, but a worried one as well. She thinks that one day I'll take just one step too many; go after just one work of art too many. Like being married to a Grand Prix racing driver, I suppose, waiting for the odds to produce their inevitable catastrophe. Like Yvonne Aubicq must have with Grover-Williams and his Bugattis, even though it wasn't the car racing that did for him in the end; just the taking of risks, much bigger and bigger risks. Which is what he must have liked.

'Those photographs, Tim: they've really upset you, haven't they?' Sue had changed her expression to a softer look. 'They're horrible things. You can't bring yourself to think of Ted Murphy in the same way at all, can you?'

I didn't answer immediately. I took a sip of black coffee. I suppose that in matters of public sexual deportment, I tend towards the French point of view. You can be as cynical as you like, condone as immoral and as decadent behaviour as you like in private, but a public façade is essential. That's not just hypocrisy, that's a question of protection. Protection of the inno- cent. Or the uninformed. I hated those photographs with a deadly hatred. If there was one thing I'd never forgive Ted Murphy for, it was those photographs. Yet in a way, I understood them. They were his private vice. There are many other vices a lot worse and you don't get a shotgun blast for them. But the most important thing was to prevent them from damaging someone innocent in an irretrievable manner. Which I supposed Will Cook and his assistants would try to do, but the odds favoured disaster for someone.

Sue was unnerved by my silence. 'Tim, you know, they'll probably find out who they all are anyway.'

'Oh, if only they would! That'd clear a hell of a lot up. But it's too much to hope. I almost wish the album could be burnt and forgotten.'

'And destroy what might be vital evidence?'

'I know that. But it's a terrible thing to confront someone with. It could destroy people's lives.'

'They might all know. Their husbands, I mean. It might all be out in the open and forgiven, as something in the past. You don't know. Even if they're recent they might have modern, open, tolerant marriages.' She grinned suddenly. 'Unlike ours.'

'Bloody right!'

'Still the same, is it?'

I nodded. 'You have an affair with someone else and I'll kill you. And him.'

She responded almost happily. 'I think you would, too.'

'Bloody right!'

'And what if I'd kill you likewise?' Her eyes were still smiling.

'Sure you would.'

'Old Testament stuff, eh, Tim?'

'Bugger the Old Testament. I'm just telling you.'

'Same here.'

'Good.' I took a cheerful sip of my brandy. 'Well, now that we've got the basis of our marriage clearly restated, what the hell am I going to do about staying alive and that lot up at Crockingham?'

'Tim, you must go very carefully and let the police do their stuff. There's nothing else you can do. As for the Collection, that's out of your hands, too. You have to just go very carefully through the motions. Recognize that you're just a pawn in this game.'

'Some pawn.'

She grinned again. 'How you hate to be manipulated. Or to be kept in the dark. I think that upsets you more than someone trying to kill you, to blow you up. If you knew their motives you'd probably forgive them. They say that to understand is to forgive.'

'Well, I wouldn't guarantee that. But you're right in one respect: the motives are what I don't understand. Someone – before I had seen those photographs of Ted's – thought that I was a danger to them. The danger must have been to do with Ted's approach to me.'

'Not necessarily. It could have been Elizabeth Dennison's approach.'

'You mean someone heard her on the phone?'

'Why not?'

'I didn't think there was anyone there. She did drop her voice, though. Perhaps she heard someone coming.'

'So you see – there's a lot to work out, yet.' Sue finished her brandy. 'Come on, Tim. I want you home with me safely before there are any more funerals to attend.'

'I must say,' Jeremy White's voice was plaintive as he swung his Bentley Continental off the M25 and headed it up the M11 motorway in the direction of Cambridge, 'that things do seem to be getting more than a little out of hand.'

I didn't reply to that. I was seated in the comfortable, passenger's leather armchair that furnishes the front of the Bentley, next to his equally comfortable driving seat. We were both dressed in solemnly subfusc suiting unenlivened by white shirts and black ties. The funereal mood suited my feelings entirely.

'I mean,' Jeremy's voice was still pitched high, 'it is quite enough to have the IRA blowing sections of the City into splinters from time to time without having to put up with the possibility of personally-oriented booby-traps being placed under one's vehicle. An expensive vehicle of which one is quite fond.'

'Indeed. As I am of mine.'

My response did not mollify him. 'I really do think it is utterly reprehensible of Uncle Richard to dodge the funeral and send you in his place like this. Under the circumstances, he should have come himself. You should be in purdah until these matters are resolved. One could be caught up in a lethal situation.'

'I did look under the car for you.'

'All the same.'

'There is no danger to you, Jeremy,' I said irritably. 'At least, not so far.'

'So far? So far? What do you mean, so far?'

'I mean,' I said, determined not to assuage his alarm in any way, 'that it does not appear, at this juncture, that the murderer or murderers yet see you as a threat to them.'

'Yet? Yet? Me? What do you mean, yet? Why me?'

'Who knows? I certainly don't. You may just do something, take some action or another, make a remark out of place, however unwittingly, that will convince Chummy and/or

Chummess that you are a threat to them, him or her. It has happened to me, obviously. Why shouldn't it happen to you?'

'Oh, no! I'm not having that! That's not on the agenda.' He accelerated the Continental emphatically past a lorry loaded with beetroot or mangelwurzels or something. 'You're not putting me on any spots of that sort. This is your affair, not mine. A typical affair, too. It really is damnable, Tim, that you seem unable to make a simple investment in a work of art without inciting criminal elements to atrocious assassinations.'

'Me? Hell! Me? I like that! I had nothing to do with buying the Crockingham Collection! You were the one who egged us into the whole thing. As usual.'

His voice rose to a higher quaver. 'The Crockingham Collection? What on earth has that to do with it? Absolutely nothing. It's this scurrilous little Irishman, Murphy or Pulham, or whatever his name is, that's the cause of the whole thing. Members of the Fulham Road fornicating classes. From your abandoned past, quite obviously. Fulham, Pulham, Murphy; there's a sort of pattern to it.'

'My God!'

I let out this one exclamation of indignation then shut my mouth tightly up. There is no point in arguing with Jeremy when he's in one of these moods. No point at all. He was taking the news badly; I suppose it's all right to think of others getting murdered, but when the target is the man sitting next to you, you begin to wonder how accurate the firing is going to be.

I let things ride for a fair space. I had things on my mind.

'There's no need to sulk,' Jeremy said suddenly. We were turning off on to the A45 so as to swing north of Cambridge.

'I'm not sulking.'

'You haven't said a word the whole of the motorway.'

'I was thinking.'

'Ha! Thinking! In a brown study, more like. What about?'

'Death. Murder. Horse paintings. A village we are soon going to pass very near, called Snailwell. Obscene photographs. A birthday card with Grover-Williams and Bugattis on it. Drowning at Fen Ditton. Shotgun blasts. The Carberry attitude. What a cocktail: I've got a permanent hangover from it all.'

He became avuncular immediately. 'My dear Tim, you mustn't let these things prey on your mind like this. It's not healthy. You take too close an interest, you know. Let the police do their job.'

'That could take months.'

'None the less. It's not your job. Compose yourself this morning. We are, as representatives of the bank, attending a solemn occasion.'

'You can say that again.'

I directed him carefully towards Bury St Edmunds, noting that we passed between Newmarket and Snailwell on the way. Then he drove the Bentley quite expertly down the lanes of Crockingham and we rolled cautiously to a halt near the church.

It was an odd church. I hadn't quite appreciated how round some of those East Anglian Saxon church towers are, like narrow turrets on a castle or something. It was very ancient, with walls of flint. Rain had started as we arrived and the grey drizzle suited my mood, although Jeremy produced an enormous, bright, harlequin golf umbrella from the boot of the Bentley and strode up the church path brandishing the unsuitable implement confidently while I tried to stay under its gaily-sectioned, jarring shelter without treading on his immaculately-polished black shoes.

The congregation for the funeral had pretty well all arrived and we slipped in at the back, trying to make as little disturbance as possible. Sir Andrew Carberry turned to look at us as Jeremy luridly flapped his collapsed brolly. I caught a brief expression of rigid disapproval on the congested red face as the bloodshot eyes saw me. His sons were behind him with respective wives and they didn't turn round. Jeremy and I slipped into our pew behind some other relatives dressed in black; to my right – thin, grey and spectacled – I saw Goodall from the Cambridge police. He nodded faintly towards me in implicit greeting.

The coffin arrived and the service took place.

No one enjoys a funeral.

When it was over, we filed out into what was now a downpour to watch the coffin being lowered into the ground as a vicar intoned. My memory of that part is confused. Eventually, we moved off to offer our respects and condolences to Sir Andrew and the family, who stood in line outside to receive us, surrounded by gravestones. Umbrellas tangled the ceremonials. There was a local newspaper photographer who fluttered nervously about, shielding his camera from the rain. Jeremy and I kept to the back of the shuffle. I found Goodall at my elbow, looking as sepulchral as a thin bespectacled policeman attending *pompes funebres* is capable of looking.

'You can collect your car,' he murmured in my ear. 'The forensic team have finished with it and I've cleared its release with DCI Roberts. It's at the police station in Cambridge. Keys with the duty sergeant.'

'Thank you very much. I must say I'll be glad to have it back,' I murmured in return. 'Anything significant come up from it?'

He shook his head. 'Only that the device was electrical. Wired to the ignition. Good job the engine wasn't started.'

'I entirely agree. Explosive?'

'Petrol. You'd have gone up in flames.'

'Charming.'

He opened his mouth, then looked round cautiously. 'Good job you did your searches yesterday,' he murmured. 'At this Murphy's shop, I mean.'

'Oh? Why?'

'There was a break-in there last night. Place was done over.'

'Good grief! What did they take?'

'Cook says they don't seem to have got anything very much. But they turned it over all right. Hell of a mess. They broke the door glass to do it. Mind you, it's not uncommon in the Fulham Road, I gather.'

'No, it's not. What about the flat above?'

'They tried that, but Cook had fully locked the mortice, et cetera, when you left. They didn't crack it. Either that or they were disturbed.'

'But they didn't take anything?'

'Nothing much, he said on the blower this morning.'

'That's a bit sinister. I wonder what the hell they were after?'

Goodall shrugged, shook his head, compressed his lips and made a gesture of caution. We were approaching the family line.

When it came to our turn, an isolated Sir Andrew, who must have been a widower or perhaps divorced, was gruffly welcoming to Jeremy, saying how much he appreciated his presence. He then nodded coolly but without hostility to me. I gave him Sir Richard's respects and moved on, trying to catch up with the gaudy shelter of Jeremy's golf umbrella.

James and his wife came next. I was prepared for James, who

looked a bit healthier in dark clothes, even though he was clearly his robust father's son, but not for his blonde wife, who looked slim and attractive. I had imagined something much horsier and more blown, but she gave no hint of bucolic pursuits. How often, I thought, one wonders how these partnerships come about; she's much too good for him.

Then came Philip, looking drawn and worried as before. Mourning seemed to suit him. He took our hands in a tight shake and murmured things about how grateful he was for our help. But by that time I hardly heard a word he said. I was staring at his wife in horror.

I knew where I'd seen her before.

In Ted Murphy's album. The second one.

It couldn't be a mistake; she was utterly recognizable, even to the colour of her hair under her black hat − they'd been colour photographs − and the set of her eyes, somehow not quite central in her face the way all eyes are supposed to be, but in this case quite noticeably off line, even with drops of moisture on her pale, untampered skin.

I'd seen her before all right.

It was such a shock that I must have stood gaping for a moment before I pulled myself together and shook her hand, almost missing her grasp through lack of focus. Her eyes briefly held mine as though seeking something, then flicked away as I muttered banal condolences and quickly moved along. I didn't want to look. I couldn't look back to check. I wanted to believe I'd made a mistake. Every feeling I could feel was going into shock. I followed Jeremy blindly down the church path to a lych gate for a moment of shelter from the wet, mind reeling and vaguely agreeing with him about not wanting to impose on the family by accepting their invitation to go back to the Hall for some sort of damp gathering and refreshments, but rather moving on to an inn somewhere, having done what was expected of us, for a proper lunch. However, Jeremy said, *noblesse oblige* and all that sort of thing, our presence is expected, so we'll have to go up to the Hall.

I must have agreed with him, regretfully, but I don't remember that part very well. I stared at last back up the path to take a distant, confirmatory stare at the family group with my eyes fixed glassily in my head. I was like a zombie.

So much like a zombie that I didn't hear the next voice that spoke to me and it had to repeat itself closer to, with Jeremy turning to frown at me for having gone deaf or stupid or something.

'– so very pleased about the decision.'

I stared blankly at the speaker. It was Frank Hobart, the brown countryman, dressed in a grey herringbone suit this time, smiling gently and holding forth his hand under the squeezed lych gate shelter where others were also trying to gather. I took the hand automatically.

'It's a great relief to know it will stay here,' he said, pumping strongly.

He must be talking about the Crockingham Collection; I managed to rally myself for a moment.

'Oh, yes. I'm pleased we were able to make a suitable offer.' I avoided Jeremy's eye as I spoke, and gestured at him. 'This is Jeremy White, by the way, who you largely have to thank. Jeremy, this is the curator, Frank Hobart. He looks after the Collection.'

Jeremy smiled widely and put his brolly to one side as he moved forward in the crush to do his Patron of the Arts impersonation. I stood reeling slightly while they shook hands and Jeremy said something about a mutually advantageous arrangement and long relationships.

Philip Carberry's wife; his bloody wife; what the bloody hell was I going to do?

'– you to meet my wife, Angela?'

Hobart's voice cut into my thoughts. Jeremy had turned beside me, umbrella slightly blocking my view. When he moved back, Mrs Hobart was standing in front of me, hand proffered forward.

Oh, God. Oh, no. Please, no.

She was much younger than her husband. Still in her forties. A strand of damp hair had come loose and was streaking her forehead. It was like a nightmare. Her fair face looked straight into mine. That strand of hair must often do that; especially in moments of physical passion. I wanted to wake up and find myself at home with Sue warm in bed beside me, but I couldn't. I was wide awake, looking at the blonde from the Portobello Road. The one whose clothes, when she had them on, I had thought American. They weren't now; she wore a black suit of English cut, not particularly flattering. In the second album, she hadn't worn anything at all. Like Ted. Like Philip Carberry's wife, what was her name? Paula. I was going into dementia.

I don't know how I shook hands, smiled, made some cliché or another leave my lips, but I did.

I did it.

I also managed to tell Frank Hobart I'd soon be in touch with him officially, once the sad ceremonies were over and we could get down to detail. He nodded, looked at me curiously, and said he'd look forward to that. They would be going back to the house now to see that arrangements for the reception of the guests were all in place.

I said something about seeing him there.

The rain quickened its remorseless cascade. Jeremy said something about dashing to the car.

I walked quickly away with Jeremy, waited for him to unlock the car, got in, sat down, and put my head in my hands behind the raindrop-dappled windows where I hoped people couldn't see me clearly.

If there'd been a bomb under the Bentley I wouldn't have noticed.

Not even if it had gone off.

CHAPTER 21

I have never attended a cheerful wake. People say that in Ireland, or New Orleans, or somewhere like those sorts of places, a wake can turn into a rave-up with music and laughter and jollity, but I've never met anyone who's had that experience. Especially not when the lamented has been murdered. It could be that one day I'll go to a reception after a funeral and find that everyone agrees that Dear Old Charlie or Great Aunt Mildred, recently squashed by a bus, had a marvellous life, no regrets, a splendid innings, and champagne will flow, jokes will crack and knickers drop like there was no tomorrow, but I doubt it.

Crockingham Hall certainly wasn't going in for any festivities when we got there.

We were allowed to enter by the front door this time, Jeremy leaving his golf brolly behind as we dodged in out of the rain. We found ourselves in a dark, panelled hall, which in this case meant a proper entrance hall with chintzy armchairs, a fireplace full of logs and a hearth bristling with black ironwork. A couple of primitive paintings of horses hung on the walls, the sort in which an arthritic animal stands in a stable with a sneer on his face, looking at a cat and three hens. There was a Turkoman rug in the entrance and a geometric Kazak in front of the fireplace. All very cosy for a transitory part of the house and intended to set the right tone as you walked in. Frank Hobart came out of a door to the left and asked us to come through, so we followed him into a long plastered room with a beamed ceiling, an inglenook and a huge oak refectory table, too long to be genuine, down the middle of it. I guessed that this was the formal dining room. The table was set out with glasses and cold food. Around it, people had already started to collect, murmuring quietly and sipping at something weak or improving to health as though they would never dream of swallowing a powerful belt of what they really needed in these circumstances. In a way, it brought the late Elizabeth Dennison more strongly to mind; I thought that she would have viewed the scene very sardonically and, *sotto voce*, would have had a memorable observation to make.

'Please help yourselves to something to drink,' Frank Hobart said. 'I have to see to the other arrivals.'

He gave me a brief, concentrated stare before he disappeared, as though seeking reassurance. Jeremy and I helped ourselves to a glass of white wine. I wished I could have had that intended conversation with the departed, not just because she had seemed interesting, alluring and unconventional. There were several mysteries she might have solved, including the intricacies of life at Crockingham Hall which were, it was clear, more complex than surface appearances conveyed. Thinking about Elizabeth Dennison like that made her – in a very minor way – immortal, I suppose. Someone you might recall frequently in times to come.

Whereas I had two very live, mortal other men's wives to think about, then and there, even though I didn't want to.

'There's no need to look quite so shattered, dear boy,' Jeremy whispered to me reprovingly. 'It's a sad occasion but it's not as though she was *close*, so to speak. For heaven's sake, pull yourself together. You look awful. You'll attract attention if you're not careful. I've given Sir Andrew assurances, you know. I don't want him getting all suspicious about your presence at Fen Ditton again.'

'Sorry, Jeremy. I'm feeling a bit below par today.'

'Below par! That's putting it mildly. You look as though you'd run into Banquo's ghost.'

I was about to retort that since I had found Elizabeth Dennison's waterlogged body only a day after meeting her, I might be entitled, more than anyone else, to distressing, sepulchral or macabre feelings of some sort, but he had already turned towards the doorway as tyres crunched on the drive. 'Ah, here they all come. The family, I mean. Try to show sympathy but for heaven's sake don't overdo it; it's awfully bad form. We'll withdraw as soon as a decent interval has elapsed.'

He moved slightly away from me towards the arriving Carberrys and I was left to watch them file in, seeing them respond to the greetings of the other people in the room with a sort of numb detachment. Gradually, as the place filled, I had to move further and further back. Jeremy was drawn away to a bay window by Sir Andrew, who got him into deep discussion. There seemed no reason for me to join them, although it would have helped if there had been; I was trying not to look round at Paula Carberry and Angela Hobart with anything other than normal courtesy rather than with hypnotized fascination or morbid curiosity.

I mean, it's not as though you meet the participants in those sorts of photographs at every old funeral you go to.

It was requiring enormous effort not to stare. Paula Carberry stood in a group which included Philip and James Carberry, talking quietly but steadily, occasionally glancing round at their guests and moving off to speak to one or two before rejoining their own group. They looked like a perfectly normal family, gathering together at a formal family occasion of loss. I wished I wasn't there. I wished I knew what to do: telling Goodall about my discoveries was somehow impossible then and there. Looking round, I couldn't see him anyway, so guessed he hadn't been asked back to the Hall. I could perhaps brace myself to inform Sergeant Will Cook or Nobby tomorrow, but action right now, at that gathering, was impossible unless it was forced upon me.

I found myself – mentally – gently cursing at Sir Richard White. What strange, hypersensitive instinct had led him to send me here today in his place?

I lost sight of Angela Hobart. She wasn't with the family group, which was understandable, and had been attending to something her husband asked her to arrange which took her briefly from the room. She must be behind me somewhere.

'Penny for them.'

Her voice in my ear practically made me jump. I managed to hold my glass with both hands and swing round not too violently to face her. She looked straight back, but the voice had been low, as though she wanted her words to carry no further than me. She used the same volume as she spoke again, not waiting for my answer.

'They must be very deep. Your thoughts, I mean. You look as though you're not here at all.'

She was familiar, yet her words were calculated to put me on the defensive. I managed to smile slightly and affect a sort of nonchalance. 'Perhaps I wasn't. Funerals tend to induce thoughts which are a bit less than superficial. In me, anyway.'

I took a sip from my wineglass as I finished speaking and looked at her over the top of it. She was an attractive sight, despite the black dress, poised evenly on her feet and looking at me without flinching. Her yellow hair seemed more noticeable inside than it had out, at the churchyard. Her eyes were blue. She had a good colour, but she wore make-up over the fine lines on her face. Her figure was mature, rounded, a little fuller than the photographs, as though country life had filled her out. Her expression was intelligent as she scanned my own expression. She knows, I thought, she bloody well knows, and now she knows that I know she knows.

'Good news about the Collection.'

She made it a statement, raising her voice a little so that someone passing us, someone I hadn't noticed, could hear. The raising produced a slight accent, hard to identify. But the remark was an irrelevance. The poise, I noticed, was one of expectation, even of tension. She was waiting for an initiative.

'Yes. Do you like it?'

She blinked flutteringly as though I had said something suggestive. Her eyelashes were long.

'Like what?'

'The Collection. Frank obviously does. He comes from a horse-painting family, doesn't he?'

'Oh. Yes, I do. Well, some of it. Frank is absolutely besotted with it, of course.'

'He must be relieved that it's going to stay here.'

'Oh yes, he is.'

All that pretence, I suddenly thought, all that pretence when I first came up here, about not upsetting Frank Hobart, that pretending to be doing an insurance check. That was to make Frank seem like an innocent outsider. Bloody rubbish. Even Mr Goodston knew, the minute that I walked through the door, that the Crockingham Collection was up for sale. Why else would I be there?

'He must have known all along that it was going to be sold, mustn't he?'

She frowned slightly. 'I – I'm not sure.'

'For how long did he know?'

'As I say: I really don't know.'

I nearly said that I didn't believe her, but more people pressed near us then moved away, talking more animatedly as the atmosphere lightened a little. I caught sight of Jeremy quickly glancing towards me with a flashed expression of concern while listening to Sir Andrew, whose back was turned in my direction.

'Look,' I said, low and quickly, 'I have to talk to you privately. About Ted.'

Her face went immobile, not shocked or stiff, but just immobile, waiting.

'Will you?'

'Yes, of course. Where?' she asked.

'Do you have a car?'

She nodded, still expectant.

I had to think quickly. 'I'm picking up my car in Cambridge, now. I suggest Snailwell. By the church. Can you get there?'

She nodded. 'When?' Still no expression. The voice low.

'This afternoon. Say at two-thirty?'

A slight hesitation. Then another nod.

'You know where it is?'

She allowed herself just the flicker of a smile. 'Oh, yes. I know.'

'Good.' I didn't ask how. It wasn't the time for that.

I moved off. I had noticed that the Carberry family group were starting to take an interest in our conversation and I went straight to them, feeling my heart beating irregularly. But I was in positive mood now that shock was dissipating into action. Something was at last happening, or was going to happen. Things might be resolved.

I smiled at Philip, nodded deferentially to James, smiled at both their wives. I made some sympathetic remark or another. They murmured bland replies, not referring to my part in the discovery of the body. Somehow Elizabeth Dennison's death seemed a taboo subject now that the church part was over. I certainly didn't want to talk about it, or get into speculations on what the police were doing.

'I expect you'll be up here more often, Tim?' Philip asked. 'When all this is resolved. For the Collection, I mean.'

'I expect so. Although once the formalities are completed there'll be little need for me to come more than once in a while. I'm sure the place can be run as it has before.'

150

'Formalities?' James Carberry's brow creased in query. 'What sort of formalities?'

'I mean the purchase formalities. There'll be quite some legal paperwork to do in this case, I imagine. It's the first full collection we've bought.'

James Carberry raised his eyebrows. 'Just a purchase contract, I should have thought.'

'Oh? I haven't been told who owns the Collection, you see. A company, isn't it?'

Philip Carberry nodded. 'Yes. I shouldn't think that will cause many complications, Tim. But I take your point about legal paperwork; it's amazing how lawyers can make work for themselves.'

'Sure.' A thought had suddenly occurred to me. 'I suppose you're all directors of the owning company, are you?'

There was a silence. For a moment they seemed reluctant to speak.

'I think we all are,' James said, rather grudgingly. 'You may find it casual of us to be uncertain, but Father has us as directors of so many companies, you see.'

I smiled. 'I'm sure. Well, we can leave those sorts of things to the accountants. And the lawyers.'

'Indeed. Thank heavens we can.'

I found that Paula Carberry was staring at me closely with her off-line eyes. She still looked pale. 'It must be very interesting,' she said, 'to make these acquisitions for your Fund.'

I forced myself to look at her. 'Yes. Yes, it is.'

She was the antithesis of Angela Hobart. Her hair was dark. Her eyes were brown. She stood awkwardly.

'Do you have to travel a lot to see things?'

Her voice was higher pitched than the other's. It was better educated. Her clothes fitted well. She looked smart. The wife of a man who made money, or a woman who had money herself.

'Quite a bit. It depends. Sometimes the auction houses have more than enough to keep us busy.'

'Do you buy much from dealers?'

The question was put without tension or particular emphasis. I noticed, though, that the others were watching me quietly.

'We buy some things from dealers, yes. It depends. They often have access to things it would be difficult for us to acquire by other means.'

151

She nodded slightly, as though I had confirmed something important rather than stating, as I thought, the obvious. However significant, right now, the obvious might be.

'Do you have a sort of approved list or do they just approach you at random?' James's voice was, as usual, more aggressive.

The four of them seemed to be waiting for my reply.

'A bit of both. We have dealers from whom we regularly buy because they know what we want and have us in mind when they're on to a particular thing. We do get cold calls though, too. It happens.'

'With any success?'

I nodded. 'Sometimes.'

'You're very circumspect.' James's rasp made it sound as though he were dealing with a civil servant. 'I don't suppose you'll cite any examples.'

'I don't think I should.'

Philip crinkled his eyebrows slightly, as though the reply perplexed him. James stared at me full on in his bold way. His wife, the slender and sophisticated woman I had been surprised by in the churchyard, smiled broadly.

'Bad luck, James. No insider info or dealer tips from this man.'

'Ha!' James Carberry grunted. 'I'm in no state to buy art works. Not until Lloyds pays out.'

'If ever,' his wife said, drily. She moved off towards a couple to our left and engaged them in conversation. The others stood irresolute for a moment and then dispersed.

I found Jeremy at my elbow.

'Good man, Tim. Saw you doing your stuff. We can slip away now. Unless you fancy cold ham and salad?'

'Not really.'

'Good. No need to take leave of Sir Andrew. I've done that for you.'

'Thank you, Jeremy.'

'He much appreciated our attendance. Not quite as anti towards you as before.' He licked his lips. 'We can stop somewhere on the road for a bite. You look washed out; you need to keep up your strength, you know.'

I was about to refuse but then I saw his expression, full of mute appeal. I sighed.

'All right, Jeremy. But no rich Burgundies; just a quick pie and a pint. And only if you drop me off afterwards at the Cambridge nick. I want to pick up my car.'

'Oh? It's ready, is it? You mean you'll go on alone from there?'

I nodded emphatically. 'Yes, Jeremy. I'll be going on alone. From there.'

The approach to Snailwell, once you turn off the A45 dual carriageway, is through impeccably-groomed fields in which expensive horses graze quietly. It is an extremely ordered landscape; even the fences and hedges look brushed. Here and there stands an estate house or a set of stables with half-doors latched uniformly open in ranks, as though an army officer was due to make an inspection. Everything conveys an overwhelming impression of money. As I swept down the long road to the village in my happily-reclaimed XJS, two men were strimming and mowing the deep green of the roadside sward, carefully cropping what elsewhere would have been tangled growth. Another was power-trimming the top of a hedge to knife-like precision.

The rain had cleared and the sun had come out to shine on a damp, freshly-washed world, looking as though men had been at work, too, in response to instructions to clean the dust off and freshen everything in sight. The funereal atmosphere of the morning was evaporating fast.

This was the kind of environment in which Alfred Munnings, racehorse painter, worked so often in England and France and America, usually staying as a guest in great country houses on the spot. The fragrant smell of mown grass would waft to his nose as he listened to the whinny of fine pedigree fillies. Stable boys and jockeys patiently held or sat on proud animals as he worked at his easel out of doors. It was a world of powerful and wealthy men for whom a horse portrait by the best artist available was yet another tangible sign of success. Port and champagne and the best claret flowed Munnings's way. His patrons smoked cigars and wore appropriate, well-cut clothes from extensive wardrobes. They owned costly motor cars and went to Monte Carlo or Nice for the season. They were aristocrats and self-made men whose possessions reinforced their self-esteem.

Gamesters too, male and female; people for whom a searing gamble was exciting and important, more important than safety and security and life's steady, tedious progressions. Small wonder that the country miller's son, expensively commissioned by them, became a minor version of his clients.

Sue would say that what he did had nothing to do with art, but most English people would disagree. Munnings was very talented, technically proficient, hard-working. He illustrates that drive for pictorial impression combined with composition and atmosphere which is so admired in England and which Whistler mocked so wittily. Munnings's admirers have not diminished.

I turned down an incline, following my instincts towards the tiny village centre, past council houses so well-tended they seemed to belong to some other category of dwelling, and rolled past new houses and a flint wall to turn left into the brief lane that passes the church.

It is another East Anglian church of great age, set behind a low flint and brick wall surrounding the graveyard, having a strange, almost tubular flint tower of modest diameter and dark, knurled flint walls punctuated by the Gothic tracery of the windows. Beyond was a paddock and a deep depression with a pond set at the bottom. Horses patrolled among the trees below that side, but a farmhouse, barn and cottage faced the church from across the open lane. Set back further on, a big old house with a Georgian façade may have been the original rectory.

Somewhere in that field above the farm to my left, seventy years ago, Munnings had painted 'Sergeant Murphy and The Drifter' in front of a clunch wall, with this church and one of the farm's buildings behind the two famous animals.

I drew up carefully, then reversed to point the nose of my car out of the lane, so that the church was on my left now and the buildings to my right. If a quick getaway was needed I was set the right way. It was twenty-five-past two so I got out to stretch my legs for the five minutes that remained and massaged a stiff knee, legacy of the collapse of a rugger scrum long ago, as I grinned into the warm sunlight.

Round the corner into the lane came a pocked yellow Lada saloon with a noisy exhaust. It seemed to waver for a moment, then it saw me and drove towards me more confidently, drawing up in front of my car nose to nose, so that any idea I might have had of driving off unimpeded ended there. The door opened and Angela Hobart got out, tossing her fair hair straight as she stood upright and looked at me.

She had changed from her funeral gear and was wearing jeans and a sweatshirt. The casual clothes looked better than the black dress; she seemed more self-assured and her figure filled the slacker clothes athletically. The sweatshirt had a motif on it I recognized as American; it was faded with genuine age, not a fashion-induced treatment.

'Hello,' I said, inadequately.

'Hello.'

She answered quietly, standing in that poised way I had noticed at Crockingham; secure yet springy on her feet. The voice, though quiet, was firm.

I gestured at the cars. 'Would you like to sit inside the car or would you prefer to stroll round the churchyard?'

I wasn't sure how clandestine she wanted our meeting to be, how hidden, although I assumed there'd be no one at Snailwell to watch or observe us.

She looked round for a moment, glanced at the now fine sky of a summer afternoon and said, 'I'd rather stroll. The funeral and that reception needs blowing away with some fresh air. At least the weather's better now. Not that I don't know this churchyard well enough.' She smiled ruefully. 'I've already done enough sitting – and more – inside cars around Snailwell to last me for ever.'

I couldn't help raising my eyebrows. The candid remark was disarming.

'With Ted?' I asked.

She nodded. 'With Ted. That's what you want to talk about, isn't it?'

'Yes.'

There was a silence for a moment, so I opened the gate and she walked through, between the yews that lead to the church door before turning off to the right, into the rather bare grass fronting the body of the building. There were few tombstones here and the feeling was of an open lawn rather than a churchyard.

'He liked you,' she said, turning to look at me. 'He talked about you from time to time. Quite a bit, now that I think of it. I think he rather envied you your job.'

'Ted? Really? He never let on. Not in that way. We always

had very good conversation, but that was it. He kept his secrets to himself.'

She smiled. 'Good conversation and secrets. Yes, that was Ted. I met him when I came back from the States. I married and went over there, but it didn't work out. When I came back I went down to the Portobello Road one Saturday morning, at a loose end, and Ted picked me up.' She smiled reminiscently. 'He was a bold charmer, was Ted. He was doing some deal with a stallholder over a bit of silver and I was watching just out of interest when he turned to me and asked me if I liked the piece enough to buy it. I was flustered; I didn't know anything about silver; but he made me laugh. Afterwards he bought me a coffee.' She shrugged. 'That was it.'

'How long ago was that?' Questions I wanted to ask were crowding into my mouth but I had to hold them back; it was not the time to press too hard, not yet.

'Oh, five or six years. We had something of a fling, then it died down.'

'Was that when he took the photographs?'

We had reached the corner of the church building. She turned to look at me seriously. Her face had closed.

'Photographs?'

'In the Portobello Road. In his album.'

'Oh.' Her face cleared a bit. 'Yes. They must have been when we first met. I often met him at the Portobello market then.'

'And the others?'

'Others?' Her voice sharpened.

'Photographs. In his other album.'

I looked directly at her. Her colour had heightened slightly, but not very much. You couldn't call it a blush. She didn't reply.

'He seems to have been a complex character,' I said. 'I didn't know him that well, I now realize.'

We turned the corner of the nave to walk round the back of the church. She shook her head.

'He wasn't complex. Oh, he had a strong drive. Great charm. Utter deviousness. But he was just another little boy lost, really. Even his name wasn't his. That's why he came up here so unexpectedly one day. Looking for Pulham. His origins. That's around the time when we met again.'

'But you knew? About the other album?'

She bit her lip. Then she nodded. 'I knew. The others didn't, according to him. It was a sort of excitement between us at first. After my failed marriage in the States I was in a throwaway mood, you see. You know how it is. Or perhaps you don't. I didn't care about anything. Nothing mattered. I might have gone to orgies, gone in for drugs. I didn't. I had Ted instead. He was all I needed. He was fun. We went to auctions together. To the races, all over the place. He loved a gamble. I didn't take him too seriously, so the album wasn't a worry at first. It was our little thrill. We were having a good time. Then it suddenly was a worry. It started to be really horrible. That sort of voyeurism gets sickening after a while. He was putting other women into the album, you see, when I wasn't around. Then he would show me them, hoping I'd be excited.'

'Is that why it ended?'

She nodded. 'That, partly. And I met Frank.'

'Where?'

'At Newmarket.' Her face clouded. 'With Andrew.'

'Carberry?'

'Yes. I was with Ted, ironically. He'd met them before somewhere. At a painting auction, I think. The London Rooms. Anyway, Frank was older and kind, more stable. His wife had died. He was still very fit for his age. At least, it seemed so. I'm not a spring chicken any more. Everything about the Carberry set-up looked good. Moneyed. Frank proposed quite quickly.'

'You mean he saw a lot of you?'

'Oh, yes. He invited me back to the races. And Ted was, well, Ted was being Ted. He couldn't change. I realized that he'd never change, never settle. He'd just drift along. That – that photography was sick. But he wouldn't give it up. Frank has an estate house and the family will always look after him. So I married him. I thought here's a chance for security.' She shook her head and a bitter expression came to her mouth. 'Out of the frying pan into the fire.'

We had turned round the path to the back of the church. There were more gravestones here, rather low, modest ones, going back to the wall separating the lower paddock.

'What went wrong?'

She bit her lip before replying. 'Frank can't, you see. Do anything of that sort. He says it was the combine accident. He's perfectly fit otherwise.' She stopped to look away towards the trees to our right and fiddled with her hands. 'I thought it wouldn't really matter. He was very nice and loved his work. He's crazy about Munnings. His ancestor painted one of Munnings's grandfather's horses or cows or something. And he's Sir Andrew's man. To the last degree.' Her voice became even more bitter. 'The very last degree. He encouraged me to help with the gallery. Sort of married couple help in a country house style. It was an attractive idea. Something to give me an interest. Very clever. I started going regularly to the Hall to work. That was when Andrew Carberry began to become attentive. His wife's in a home, you see. Has been for years. He can't divorce.' Her mouth twisted. 'So he wanted to exercise his *droit du seigneur.*'

'Oh, God!'

'Oh, it wasn't put like that. And he's very generous.'

'But what about your husband?'

'Frank? He's a loyal Carberry man. And he wasn't jealous. Not of that, as long as I stayed his wife. As long as life – his position – was secure.'

'So you agreed?' I tried not to make my tone incredulous or too prurient. My thoughts were running off in all directions. Could Frank Hobart somehow have been deliberately procuring her for his boss?

She smiled wryly. 'Oh, I resisted. But eventually I was bored. So I fell. It's hard to refuse persistent attention. In the right circumstances, of course. When you are desired like that and life is very – very local and limited. Frank away doing something for Andrew, me feeling a bit in need, no one at the Hall, that sort of thing. Champagne in a bucket. All very carefully arranged. I'm afraid I have a weakness for luxuries. And Andrew continues to be very generous, especially to Frank. It all fits together.'

'Then Ted turned up?'

She nodded. 'Then Ted turned up. Out of the blue. I went into the gallery one day and there he was, talking to Frank. He told me he had been researching his family origins at Pulham. But I think there was more to it. While Frank was out for a moment, Ted suggested we meet here, at Snailwell. I didn't know why, then; didn't know the significance of the place for him. He was his old charming self. Made me feel important, clever. Added a bit of spice to life. He could always do that.'

'So you came?'

'I came.' It was a simple statement. 'I wanted a change from Crockingham. It gets claustrophobic there.'

'And Frank found out?'

She turned to me swiftly. 'Oh, no. You don't think Frank did that, do you? Shot Ted, I mean? He couldn't.'

'Why not? A shotgun is a countryman's weapon.'

'But Frank was at home with me all that night! I swear it! He couldn't possibly have been down in London. No, it has to have been one of Ted's other girlfriend's men that did it. A husband. Ted was always one for married women. They were the ones who wanted a bit of excitement. Without Ted having to worry about marriage, like a single girl might want. A man like Ted could always get one of those.'

We had reached the other side of the church. I turned to look at her, watching the fair face creased in anxiety.

'Did you ever go back to the Fulham Road?'

She shook her head. 'Oh, no. I wasn't going back on Ted's camera. We met here, or at pubs out this way. Sometimes in Cambridge. It wasn't very often. Ted and I both had lives to lead. He liked it here, though. He said there was a painting he'd got of this place. A Munnings. It was a commission, he said. He was very affected by it. He said it personified his character. "Sergeant Murphy and The Drifter". The disciplined part of him was Sergeant Murphy. The way his life was going was The Drifter. I agreed with that. I told you; he was another little boy lost, despite all his – his adult enjoyments.'

'He said it was a commission? What for?'

She shook her head. 'I'm not sure. There was something going on that he hid from me. In his business, I mean. Ted was like all those antique dealers. Very secretive.'

I had no doubt this was true. Antique dealers are the least open of people. Ted, for reasons I now understood too well, was a paramount example.

'Well, there was a connection with Frank, then. And Frank could have planted the bomb under my car, couldn't he?'

Her eyes widened. 'I – I don't – I can't believe –'

'His army experience?'

We were round to the tower side of the church. Tombstones to my right ranked close to the paddock wall, with a drop beyond it. The yew trees along the church entrance were in front of us. A Land Rover now stood behind the yellow Lada and, as we looked, the door opened and a man got out.

It was Frank Hobart.

He must have followed her carefully.

Angela Hobart's eyes widened and she moved forward in a swift springy stride, crossing the grass to the yew trees as she called out.

'Frank?'

He reached back inside the Land Rover and pulled out a long object wrapped in a piece of blanket; a long object I recognized before he unwrapped the enveloping cloth. It was a shotgun.

A double-barrelled shotgun.

'Frank!' Her voice rose to a scream.

He fired just the once as she came between the yews about ten yards in front of him, the right barrel emitting a puff as the loud bang of the twelve bore split the silence. She was jerked backwards by the impact full in the chest, going down to strike the path surface as a slackened body already. Her right leg bounced just once before she became a crumple of sweatshirt and jeans lying on the path.

By then I was running.

A twelve bore is lethal up to about thirty yards. About the distance I was from Frank Hobart. After that it depends on the shot, the load, the place it hits. I wasn't waiting to find out. I saw Hobart swivelling in my direction and went down behind the tombstones near the paddock wall with a perfect swallow dive as the second barrel banged like a cannon and shot spattered and chipped bits of stone all round me. Then I rolled over, got my good knee under me and braced myself ready for another dash as I took a quick look.

He had moved towards me and got the gun open already. I saw the two spent cartridges eject into the air in quick fragments of red and his right hand go into his big jacket pocket. You can reload a twelve bore in seconds if you're practised. It was a good twenty-five yards to him and I'm not a gambler, as I've said. As I jumped up, his hand came out of the pocket in an easy sweep, holding two more little red cylinders. I reckoned I'd get to him at about the same moment as the gun snapped shut with two new cartridges in it. I was turning ready to wheel round for a jump over the wall into the paddock when I saw a white

Ford Sierra screech to a halt alongside the Land Rover. Out of it jumped Inspector Goodall and another man.

'Police!' Goodall shouted. 'Armed police! Freeze!'

The other man ran round the car and started bringing his hands up in the recognized clench on a weapon. Frank Hobart, startled, gun still open but cartridges inserted, looked at them, back to me, back to them.

'Drop it!' Goodall shouted. His mate crouched in a really menacing crouch, pointing what I now saw to be a pistol.

Hobart looked back towards me. I got ready to leap over the wall in the best touchline dive I could muster. The shotgun snapped shut.

He spun it round so deftly that he might have practised the exercise for years. Goodall let out another shout, but the end of it was drowned in the bang of the twelve bore. A piece of the back of Frank Hobart's head seemed to detach itself and disintegrate in a spray towards the church tower. His face held for a moment then, as his legs buckled, smudges round his mouth blossomed into red. He fell backwards and I saw the soles of his shoes cock up, twist, and keel over.

Goodall and the other man ran into the churchyard. Behind me, I heard the whinny of a frightened horse somewhere.

I sat down on a short tombstone and began to shake uncontrollably.

Before I started to vomit my pub lunch all over somebody's last resting place.

CHAPTER 23

They weren't pleased. None of them. You'd think from the way they carried on that I'd shot someone myself. I was distinctly unpopular. My own feelings were treated unsympathetically. It was all irritable hostility for hours at Cambridge Police Station, with Nobby on the phone in a filthy temper because he couldn't leave whatever he was doing and charge up to Cambridge to be nasty to me face to face. I had to put the phone down on him. The local rozzers wittered on as though I'd pinched all their carrycots. By their reckoning, I had suborned an important witness before getting her shot. They practically accused me of causing the death of her husband-murderer. I'd upset all the rules. The evidence was now hearsay, verbal, from me, a third party. An unreliable, irresponsible third party. To hear them, you'd think they would have preferred it if he'd shot me first then maybe they could have extricated the two Hobarts alive themselves.

They'd followed me from Cambridge when I collected the XJS but – and this is the real reason why they were so snotty – they lost me on the A45 because, not to be late at Snailwell, I'd speeded along then turned off after some roadworks and they missed the turn. I always suspected that Nobby had ordered them to follow me but I hadn't been sure. Goodall and his chum had virtually to ask their way to Snailwell by checking with the strimmers and hedgers along the route about who'd seen a light blue XJS go by. Hence their late arrival.

It put them in a bad light. That was what they were finding it hard to forgive.

'You should,' Goodall repeated to me grimly several times, 'have advised me that you were arranging this meeting and, additionally, kept me advised that Angela Hobart was connected – intimately – with the Murphy character. It was your duty to report that as soon as you knew, not to arrange clandestine meetings of your own with her. It is an offence to withhold information. Who do you think you are? I could charge you with obstruction.'

'You weren't there.'

'I wasn't invited to the Hall after the funeral, I agree, no. But that didn't have to stop you from keeping me informed, did it? Especially since you came here – right here to the station – to collect your car.'

I sighed. It was, I could have pointed out, only reasonable to hear Angela Hobart's version of affairs before egging the Cambridgeshire Constabulary and the Chelsea branch of the Metropolitan Police on to her, but Goodall might not have liked my saying that. He might have asked who else's story I wanted to hear before I reported such connections and I might have had to say Paula Carberry's.

Because I did want to hear it. Paula Carberry's version, I mean.

Before I told Goodall, Nobby or Will Cook about it.

It seemed only fair to me.

I could always plead that I wasn't absolutely sure about the photographs being of the same people. I mean, they weren't exactly studio portraits. One has to give people the benefit of the doubt. I'm not a policeman, after all.

Sue absolutely agreed with me.

'You'll have to see Paula Carberry,' she said, once I was back at the flat in Onslow Gardens and had told her the whole story. 'It's too serious a thing to just blurt out to anyone like the police. It could ruin her life. All the Carberrys' lives. Philip Carberry is the most decent of them all. How on earth she got involved with Ted Murphy I can't imagine. Through the Hobarts, I assume. I think he must have been a sort of Rasputin. But what a horrifying set-up. That Angela Hobart qualifies as a scarlet woman in many ways, but I can't help feeling sorry for her. The arrangements at Crockingham Hall are really too unpleasant to think about. Those awful men. Poor girl; she was trapped into it, really.'

She was being very charitable, but then she wasn't personally involved. It seemed to me that Angela Hobart was, like Ted Murphy, one of life's opportunistic drifters; in her case a sybaritic as well as an unlucky one. What she had told me about Frank Hobart and Ted Murphy being together in the gallery had my mind racing. I tried to work out a connection with Elizabeth Dennison too, but apart from the obvious crossings of the two women's lives, Elizabeth Dennison had not come into anything that Angela Hobart had said. The real reason why her husband had shot her – if jealousy was eliminated and I wasn't sure it was – didn't seem clear to me yet. The answer lay at Crockingham Hall somewhere. And I was in bad enough odour with the Carberrys already; I wasn't in shape to go asking.

Jeremy made all that very clear the next morning. He summoned me so peremptorily to his office that Penny came in white-faced to deliver the command, looking at me as though the tumbril was waiting.

'For heaven's sake!' he hollered, glaring at me from behind the fortification of his desk. His face was as congested as I've ever seen it. 'What on earth were you up to? I can't leave you for five minutes! I've never heard such fury from Sir Andrew! The phone nearly exploded. His faithful man, years of service, goes out after the funeral, finds you chatting up his wife in another churchyard somewhere and shoots her and himself! The police say you say that she was his mistress! He's beside himself!'

'Who?'

Apart from not twitting Jeremy on his bad syntax, I was avoiding pointing out that I, too, had been an intended victim in Snailwell churchyard. It didn't seem to me to be the moment to make that point; he might not have expressed any sympathy.

'You know damned well who I mean! He denies absolutely that there was any impropriety between himself and Angela Hobart! He's going to sue you! He may even sue the bank. He doesn't even like to accept your word that she was so close to Ted Murphy.' Jeremy put on a grudging expression. 'Although the police have confirmed that, apparently, from photographic comparison of their own.'

'I'm glad to hear someone believes me. He can't sue, by the way.'

'Don't avoid the issue! Stop prevaricating! We're going to lose the whole account! Do you realize that? He says that it's clear that Hobart shot Murphy in jealousy and then shot his wife and himself in the bargain. Especially finding her with you like that. A domestic affair. In which you have played all too prominent a role! And you are trying to implicate Sir Andrew in it! Coming

165

on top of your suspicious presence in the Elizabeth Dennison affair, it's the absolute limit! He wants no more to do with a bank that employs you.'

'Oh, really? A domestic affair, eh? Just jealous old Frank Hobart at work, eh? When he was a complaisant husband for God knows how long at Crockingham? Who tried to blow me up in my car? Who clubbed and drowned Elizabeth Dennison and ransacked Ted Murphy's shop? All very domestic, I must say.'

'What on earth are you trying to say now? What mad theories are these? For God's sake! I simply can't take the responsibility for you in these sorts of circumstances! You're obsessed! Unhinged. Your use of the Art Fund, your behaviour, is destroying the bank's custom. The directors will want action.' His rounded eyes whitened significantly. 'Immediate, executive action!'

'Including Sir Richard?'

He blinked, spoiling his glare. 'What do you mean, including Sir Richard? What has Uncle Richard got to do with this madness? He's in France.'

'From whence you brought him over, Jeremy.'

'So?'

'Richard,' I said patiently, feeling inclined to use a phrase like 'hoist by your own petard' or similar, but in the circumstances resisting temptation, 'clearly smells a rat of some sort in the Carberry farmyard. Hence my presence.' I shook my head sadly at him. 'You should know by now, Jeremy, that Richard does not substitute me for himself except in circumstances of deep suspicion. And possible violence.'

'Violence is right! Absolutely right! It clings to you like filings to a magnet.' He glared wildly at me, then round about him in a sort of despair. Thoughts visibly started to chase themselves across his congested expression. My words had cut deep. I have worked as Sir Richard White's pet ferret too often for Jeremy to ignore the implications. His mouth moved to form statements which did not emerge. His face worked for a moment, then fell. The whitened eyes dropped to the surface of the desk in front of him. A sort of resignation then caused his well-tailored shoulders to slump. At last, bitterly, he spoke, looking up again at me with weary resignation. 'Oh, God. I suppose this means that the Carberry account is a goner. Whatever we do.'

'I think it probably is.'

He closed his eyes. 'It couldn't have come at a worse time. Really it couldn't.'

'Courage, Jeremy. The Carberrys are probably on the verge of coming an enormous cropper.' Horse terminology is infectious. 'We may be well shot of them. Sir Andrew's reputation is not exactly pure.'

'All the same! We've handled him for years. There are substantial funds to manage.'

'Check with Richard. Tell him what's happened and ask his advice.'

Jeremy glared at me. He has never liked asking his uncle's advice, except when it suits him. Like at Art Fund meetings. 'What are you holding back? What evidence do you have?'

I shook my head. 'Regrettably, not enough. But I still have an avenue or two to explore.'

'Dear God! An avenue or two! How many more horrors will happen along these avenues before you're satisfied?'

'None, I hope. I hope I'm wrong. How's Geoffrey been getting on, by the way?'

He bridled. 'Geoffrey? Geoffrey? For heaven's sake will you keep to the point! What are you talking about now?'

'You said that Geoffrey, our excellent accountant, was checking the ownership of the Crockingham Collection. To see that our purchase is outright, freehold, whatever. So that proper title is established. How is it going?'

He waved at me irritably. 'I've no idea. Good God, that sort of technicality is the least of our worries. You really seem to have no sense of priorities! Check with Geoffrey yourself if you're so interested. Sir Andrew will almost certainly withdraw the sale to us now, anyway.'

'Don't bank on that, Jeremy.' I got up; as in the theatre, the timing of exits from Jeremy's office is important. 'Don't bank on that at all. I will go and check with Geoffrey as you suggest.'

I gave his bewildered face a respectful nod and cleared off before further eruptions took place. To my surprise, when I got to my office Geoffrey Price was already in it, bandying words with a harassed Penny. They both looked at me expectantly as I strolled in.

'How was it?' Geoffrey queried, with mock solicitude. 'Six of the best? Gated for a month? Clear your desk before tea time?

167

This hurts me more than it will you? More in sorrow than in anger?'

'Down, boy, down!' I grinned back at him. Geoffrey has a clear sense of office survival. 'But I'm pleased to see you. I was just talking about you.'

I looked at Penny, who was staring at me with a mixture of apprehension and excitement. There's nothing like an office crisis, with the threat of sacking, to give a secretary a proper frisson.

'Are you all right?' she demanded, with gratifying solicitude. 'What happened? He sounded *absolutely livid* on the phone.'

'I am all right. Thank you for your concern, Penny. I am well. Thank heavens I have powerful friends. Bring coffee and I will reveal all. In the meantime, Geoffrey, how goes the Crockingham ownership?'

Penny scurried off in relief and Geoffrey sat down with the ponderous solemnity of a true accountant.

'I thought you'd ask soon, so that's why I'm here. The Collection is owned by a company called Equestart. A combination of the words equestrian and art, you see. Very clever. I really couldn't have thought of that.' He smiled wolfishly; accountants are much given to sarcasm. 'It's a tax dodge of the Carberrys to cover the expenses. The Collection comprises the sole assets of the company and, by acquiring the shares of the company, we thus acquire the Collection.'

'Which is what?'

'What is which? I mean, what do you mean?'

'How is the Collection defined?'

'Oh, I understand. There is an inventory of the assets, as with all good companies, verified by the auditors. It is substantially the list of paintings as per the catalogue you brought back. The official visitors' catalogue.'

'What extras, variations, et cetera, are there?'

'Variations? Ah, true; perceptive of you. There are some incidental extra items, sketches, paintings and so forth, not on display. A supplementary list.'

'Also audited?'

'Er, well, yes.'

'You don't sound too sure.'

'There is a note from the auditors that says the valuations of the supplementary list are more or less OK, but since the supplementary list is of minor works of low value they haven't requested a new, detailed valuation for – let me see – three or four years. It seems these are mainly sketches and so on, even some prints and drawings.'

'How many?'

'The list comprises maybe a hundred or more items.'

My eyes widened. 'A hundred? Quite a lot.'

'Well, you know better than I do, Tim, it's like the Art Fund. You can accumulate drawers full of sketches and so on. Carberry was a prolific buyer in his heyday. Reclassifying everything in detail is a bind hardly worth spending a lot of time and expense on once you've done the original inventory. Especially if these items represent a low percentage of the total value. The auditors would probably accept a statement from the directors confirming that the list is substantially unchanged. For a while, anyway.'

'Mmm.'

'What do you mean by that dubious mmm? Ah, here's Penny with the coffee. A sight quicker than we get it, you are, down here.'

'It seems a bit slack, not to recheck that list.' I nodded cheerfully at Penny, indicating that she should pour out the coffee.

'Oh, I've no doubt it should be checked at regular intervals but we here have nothing to lose. The valuation at which we're buying the Collection is based on the main catalogue. This supplementary list is a bonus, really. If there's anything of value in it, we'll have a bonus.'

'Oh,' I said, accepting a cup of coffee. 'I don't think we'll get any bonuses. Not from the Crockingham Collection.'

Geoffrey blinked at me. Penny regarded me curiously. I smiled at their puzzlement.

'I think,' I said, 'that any bonuses were removed a while ago. Hidden. That's why someone ransacked Ted Murphy's shop. They didn't find what it was they wanted, though. It was too well concealed. For all of us.'

Penny wriggled excitedly. 'How thrilling! Hiding things and finding them is such fun. They say that you should use the obvious if you can. Like my mother's jewellery.'

We looked at her patiently; you're not supposed to be rude to junior staff these days, especially not female ones.

'Her jewellery,' she explained brightly. 'When we had a

burglary, years ago. The security people told my mother not to keep it in its box in her chest of drawers when it wasn't in the vault. Burglars always look there first. So she hung it on the mirror. I mean, necklaces and earrings and things. The burglar missed them completely. Thought it was just junk, I suppose. I mean, I don't suppose people normally hang their good stuff on the mirror, do they? So he missed it.'

'On the mirror,' Geoffrey repeated, tolerantly humouring the girl, as only a senior officer of the bank, concerned for good employee relations, especially young female employee relations, should. 'Your mother hid it by hanging it on the mirror?'

'Yes.' Penny nodded brightly.

'Remarkable.' Geoffrey tried not to sound too condescending. 'Quite remarkable.'

'Christ!' I said, putting my cup down.

'What's up?'

'The mirror. Of course. That's why he never sold it. It has to be in the mirror.'

'What has?'

I grabbed the phone to dial Chelsea.

'What we've been looking for. Or at least, I have. Orpen was famous for mirror images, too. Hello? Sergeant Will Cook, please. Thank you.' I clapped my hand over the receiver and smiled at Penny. 'You are a brilliant girl, d'you know that? Utterly and completely brilliant. A jewel. Oh, pun, sorry. Hello? Oh, it's not Will Cook, it's you. Hello, Nobby. Still skulking about at Chelsea are you? No, there is absolutely no need to be offensive. None at all. Look: can it, Nobby and listen! *Listen.* Yes, I have. No, I won't. Meet me at Ted Murphy's shop, now, and I'll tell you. No, Nobby. I said now and I meant now. *Now.*'

CHAPTER 24

'This had better be good,' Nobby Roberts said forcefully, in his most inspectorial tones, as I approached the door of Ted Murphy's shop. 'Very, very good.' He looked at his watch pointedly. 'I hope this isn't just for the exposition of another of your clever theories. Or that any further bodies will roll out of the woodwork.'

He had brought Will Cook, who was standing beside him in solid complement, and the sergeant gave me a nod of welcome that contrasted amicably with his superior's gingery scowl.

'Patience, Nobby,' I said cheerfully. 'Everything comes to he who waits. No, no further bodies.'

'What do you want to look at first?' The response was abrupt. 'The shop or the flat? We haven't time to muck about.'

'Oh, the shop. The answer to all antique and art dealers' lives is always to be found in their shops. *In commerciendum veritas*, you know, or something like that. Latin; you remember?'

His look reddened. Will Cook got out his keys. Beside us, the traffic of the Fulham Road rumbled past unheeding. A woman with a string bag, relic of pre-plastic days, carried brussels sprouts down the pavement, muttering. Will Cook swung the door open.

The gallery-shop was in worse shape than on my previous visit. The ransacking had not improved things. On the Period Wall two of the paintings hung askew like marionettes left stringbound. The stuff on the floor was badly disarranged. I stepped past the two policemen, over the bric-à-brac dislodged by the break-in and went across to Ted's desk. Above it the glass of the big splashy watercolour reflected my face back at me where the invitation cards stuck into the frame didn't obscure the surface. The frame was oversize, much more oversize than I remembered now that I was concentrating on it; the mount was very wide.

I took the frame at each corner – it was nearly four feet across – and lifted the whole ploughing scene down until it was safely on the floor behind the desk. As with so many Victorian pictures, the gilt frame was damaged and flaky but the backing of thin panelled wood was intact, screwed to the frame by small brass screws. The whole thing was heavy; much heavier than it should have been.

'Deep, isn't it?' I said out loud. 'Far deeper than you need for a watercolour, its mount, backing, anything else. That is an oil painting's frame, not a watercolour's. There's a deep space in there. Behind the picture itself, I mean.'

They came across and stood over me as I got out my penknife, opened its little screwdriver and tried one of the brass screws. It turned easily. Regular use would do that.

'You better clear the desk,' I said, since they weren't doing anything but standing watching me narrowly, making me nervous. 'We'll see more clearly there.'

They obliged, grudgingly in Nobby's case. He lifted one set of papers off and let Will Cook do the rest.

I lifted the whole frame and put it face down on the desk where it was easier to see and to get at. Then I unscrewed the brass screws. There were twelve of them. The thin panel of the backing lifted off quite freely; the sealing paper had been cleanly slit all the way round.

'Jesus!' Will Cook said, awestruck.

The space under the panel was packed with fifty-pound notes. Thick swatches of them.

In a space about three feet wide by two foot six high by nearly four inches deep you can get a lot of fifty-pound notes. They were tightly packed. Certainly a hundred thousand pounds' worth of them. Perhaps more.

'I thought you said he wasn't a blackmailer.' Nobby's tone to Sergeant Will Cook was aggrieved and accusatory; his subordinate was in danger of being verbally duffed-up.

'It's not blackmail money,' I said, lifting a pack of fifties out so that I could see behind. 'At least, I don't think so.'

'Well, what is it, then?' Nobby wasn't any friendlier. 'His pension fund?'

'Proceeds,' I responded.

'Proceeds? What do you mean, proceeds?'

'Of sales. Of supplementary works in the Crockingham Collection. And commissions.'

'Eh?'

'Proceeds, Nobby. And commissions. Ted Murphy was helping – I believe – someone at Crockingham to sell off the stock. Not the paintings on display in the gallery at the Hall – that would be too obvious – but a supplementary list. Not a very clearly defined list. The list is technically the property of a company called Equestart, along with all the rest of the inventory. It forms part of the company's assets. Any disposal of such assets, as I am sure I do not have to remind a Fraud Squad man, must be reflected in the company accounts and, subsequently, declared for tax purposes. Yes?'

'Yes,' Nobby said heavily. He and Will Cook were still staring at the money. 'Yes. Good Lord! How do you know this?'

'Ah. Well. I am not offering incontrovertible proof, not yet. I *am* saying that I am fairly certain that this is what it is. If you want to dispose of such assets, for cash, who better than an antique and art dealer to filter them out for you? To hand the cash on to you, less his commission?'

'Wait a minute.' Cook took a pack of fifties and stared at them as though they weren't real. 'You'd have to trust the dealer pretty solidly. And how do you account for the diminishing inventory back at – what was it – Equestart?'

'Ted Murphy had the gift of the gab. His contacts were good. His supplier needed money urgently. As for the inventory, you don't account for any diminishing returns. You get the dealer to provide you with substitute paintings or sketches. You replace the good stock you've taken out with duff daubs and drawings in their place so that, at stock-check, everything balances. When I looked at Ted's books the last time we were here, it struck me how ill-defined a lot of the items were. "Ploughing Scene", "Landscape with Trees", that sort of thing. No problem for Ted to provide suitable pictures to replace things taken from Crockingham.' I gestured at the walls and the stack on the floor. 'Look at 'em.'

Cook's mouth opened, closed, then opened again. 'It can't be that easy,' he protested.

'Oh yes, it can.' Nobby's voice was grim. Nobby is an experienced Art Fraud Squad man 'Oh yes, it bloody well can. Especially if the supplementary stock, as Tim calls it, is not usually on view. If it's just a spare collection of all sorts of things in drawers or racks, given a quick stock-check once a year by an obliging auditor – or more likely one of his trainees who changes every year – who knows the collection to be really the property of a rich and influential man who's hardly going to rob himself, is he?'

'Until he has to, Nobby.'

'Until he has to, Tim. To make up for losses elsewhere.'

'And in his mind they're his, anyway. To him, the company is just a technicality. It's his collection, damn it, so he'll decide what to do with it.' I was still lifting the packs of bank notes out to get to the back of the ploughing horses. A stiff card surface was gradually coming to view. The back of a watercolour is usually protected by card of that sort. Especially if you're using the space behind to stack money in.

'But surely,' Will Cook's voice was moving into an indignant mode now, 'surely – I mean – if Murphy was the goose that provided the golden eggs, why shoot the bugger?'

'Ah,' I said. 'I didn't say I could solve that. What I can do is to fill in the answer to one of the clues in the crossword puzzle. Then you've got a bit more to go on.'

'Here,' Nobby said, suddenly recalling his official position. 'This money has got to be properly collected and accounted for or there'll be real trouble. Get a bag from the car, Will.'

Cook disappeared and came back with a canvas holdall. They stacked the packs of notes carefully into it, all the while exposing the card surface below.

'I suppose that watercolour's got this card backing to protect it,' Nobby said, at last getting to the lower surface. 'They're normally on paper or card, aren't they?'

'Usually, Nobby. You can see the whole piece of card now. It fills the surface area.'

This was true. At last, most of the money was off the surface and I could carefully take the edges of the card in my fingers. Its size was almost exactly the inner dimensions of the frame. I moved it out gently. A plain canvas surface came to view behind it.

'What's that?' Nobby demanded. 'They haven't backed the watercolour with canvas, have they?'

'No, Nobby.' My heart was starting to pound. 'That is the back of a painting. An oil painting. There are two backing cards –

you see? – and the oil painting is safely sandwiched between them. A canvas, cut from its stretcher and stored face away from us. Hidden from both sides.'

'Christ!' His voice had changed tone. 'Well don't keep us gasping, you old trout. What is it? A bloody Rembrandt?'

I lifted the first card away and took the canvas carefully by the edges to lift it out. Then I respectfully turned it over and put it face up on the card.

It was an oil painting of a scene in front of a country house. In the centre was a blonde, young, bareheaded woman in riding breeches or jodhpurs, standing by a horse whose head was held by a groom. A little dog capered at her feet. Behind her was the portico of the house, a stone foreign-looking mansion with a carriage sweep. On the left was a large saloon car, a dated, square luxurious vehicle of the nineteen-twenties with a chauffeur in leggings standing by the driver's door, looking towards the horsewoman. I took all this in in one quick breathless glance. Then I looked harder at the horse: it was brown and had two white back feet and one white front one.

'Rather a modern scene,' Nobby said, disappointed. 'Not a Rembrandt at all. Nineteen-twenties? Don't think motor cars are a big artistic seller, are they?'

'It's a Rolls,' Will Cook said. 'Look at the radiator. Chauffeur's togged out in breeches, all proper. Nice horse, though.'

'That horse,' I said, finding my voice a bit thick and difficult, 'was called Sergeant Murphy. It won the Grand National in 1923.'

'Eh?'

'The lady is Yvonne Aubicq. Look at her blonde hair.'

'Aubicq? Wasn't that – wasn't that –?' Nobby has been a friend for a long time. And knows the worst.

'The chauffeur you see there was called Grover, then. He became Grover-Williams later, when he drove Bugattis.' I bit my lip. 'It's an unusual composition, I agree. Perhaps Orpen was experimenting. Or perhaps he wanted to paint the household one day, while he was in the country somewhere. It looks like France. In the early 'twenties he lived between Paris and London. Or maybe the contrast – cars taking over from horses, as Munnings so hated. Orpen has used Sergeant Murphy as his model.' I pointed to the signature at the bottom of the canvas: *Orpen*. 'This is the Orpsie Boy who noted from my telephone message on Ted Murphy's answerphone. Orpen. See it? The signature, I mean.'

I found I was getting a bit emotional at that point and shut up, perhaps a bit abruptly. The figures in the composition, caught in the painted moment, seemed to look across at each other with a precognition or premonition, or whatever the word should be, of a future that in reality only we, now, could imagine. We were imposing our hindsight on our view of the scene. At the time Orpen produced it, this was just another painting; something or another he was doing for himself instead of the endless portraits of that period. It was hard to imagine, now, that here was just a lady in a landscape with a house and a horse with groom and a car with chauffeur, the figures cleverly posed, and some trees and a sky with clouds, not the deeply significant scene that time had imprinted on our vision.

Cook had gone silent, too. Nobby went on staring with almost the same intensity as me for a while, then he spoke.

'This is it,' he said, wonderingly. 'This is the painting he sent you the birthday card about.'

'Yes.' Something was making me blink, misting the space between me and the picture. I had to rub my eyes to refocus. Fortunately, they weren't looking at me. They were still looking at the painting.

'You jammy bastard!' Nobby said. 'You strung everyone on all along until you could find this.'

'No, I didn't. Not really. But I've found it all the same.' I rubbed my face with a damp and rather grubby hand. 'There's the answer to Ted's card. There's no further role for me to play, now. My part is over.'

He swung round to face me almost ferociously.

'Oh no, you don't! You're not getting away with that!'

I blinked at him in surprise, my attention shaken away from the painting. 'What do you mean? What on earth can I do, now?'

'You,' he said, shoving his ginger features close to mine, 'can help us to secure a conviction. That's what you can do.'

'What?'

'A conviction. You. For us.'

'Me? I thought you said I was under no circumstances to become involved. You were adamant about it.'

He grinned broadly. 'It's a bit late to be using that one, Tim.'

He looked at the canvas bag full of money, the poignant figures with horse and car, and turned his vision to sweep round the tumbled surroundings of shop and street for a deliberate moment. Then he put his hand on my shoulder in an affectionate gesture he hadn't made for a long time. 'Come on, old friend. You've got what you want. You can give me the rest of it, now.'

The London address of Philip and Paula Carberry was in a mansion block of the kind used by politicians in the area of Westminster that stretches between Victoria Street and the Horseferry Road. It occurred to me, as I rang the bell, that perhaps Sir Andrew Carberry had used it in his parliamentary days and had simply passed it on to his younger son when all that came to an untimely end.

Paula Carberry responded to my ring and buzzed the opener that let me in to the hallway. From there, I took the lift up to the third floor. I've never liked the security systems of those sorts of apartment blocks, but I suppose nowadays they are essential if you don't want to lose the odd Modigliani or be held to ransom by frustrated bankrobbers.

She came out on to the landing as I drew the outer lift door back, and smiled faintly, holding out her hand for a medium-firm shake. As before, she was smartly turned out; not in mourning now but soberly clad in a dark wool dress that covered her right up to the neck.

'Please come in,' she said.

I followed her into a well-carpeted room furnished with the usual tasteful settee and easy chairs, gold mirror over a mantelpiece, paintings of flowers, good curtains and occasional small tables. It didn't look very lived-in. I guessed it would be used about four nights a week or less, when Philip had to be in town for business. The remaining nights would be spent in the country, boating down on the Hamble or away abroad on business. Beyond the settee, on the other side of the room, doors led to what were probably a bedroom with bathroom and, separately, a kitchen. I could glimpse a range of cupboards where one door was ajar. I could easily have been in a hotel suite.

'Thank you for seeing me at such short notice,' I said.

'Won't you sit down?' She gestured at one of the chairs.

'Thanks.' I sat carefully opposite her as she perched on the edge of the settee. The skew arrangement of her features and pale, untampered skin were more noticeable at close quarters. The off-line brown eyes were fixed on me intently and I found I had to stop myself from blinking or avoiding her gaze by conscious effort.

'You said it was urgent,' she said, making it plain that she was not going to take any initiatives.

'Yes. I'm sorry to intrude on what is a private matter, especially at such a tragic time, but I wanted to talk to you about Ted Murphy.'

Her face didn't change much but she made a small crinkle of a frown cross her forehead.

'Ted Murphy?'

'Yes. It's about the connection between you and him, you see.'

'Connection?' The crinkle deepened into a furrow. 'I'm afraid I don't understand.'

I pressed my hands together carefully and rubbed them in a slight handwashing motion. This wasn't going to be easy.

'I have very strong views on personal privacy. And I hate to intrude. But the relationship between you and Ted Murphy, who was, after all, helping to dispose of some of the Crockingham paintings, is a piece of knowledge only I possess. I wanted to come and see you before I did anything about it. I think that's only fair.'

She stared at me as though in disbelief. 'Ted Murphy? Me? I'm afraid I don't understand you.'

I bit my lip. 'I have to tell you that I know for certain that you were on intimate terms with Ted Murphy. This is rather an important piece of information for me alone to contend with, in the circumstances. It's giving me a difficult responsibility.'

It sounded terrible; pompous; accusatory; sanctimonious. I hated it. But I couldn't think, then and there, of any other way of saying it.

'How?'

The question was fired at me almost like a pistol shot.

'How? I'm sorry, I don't understand.'

Her voice had a sneer to it. 'How are you certain? Of my – relationship, as you call it, with Murphy?'

179

She was still bluffing it out. I would have in her place, too. It was time to destroy that bluff.

'Ted Murphy had a photograph album which – which came into my possession. In it there are photographs of you. Intimate photographs. Taken clandestinely in his bedroom. I'm afraid that he had a hidden camera.'

She had gone white. Anger and dislike made the unequal eyes widen as she spoke. 'Photographs? I don't believe you!'

I reached into my jacket, took out an envelope and handed it to her, rising to cross between armchair and settee. Then I returned to sit back. Her eyes fixed on mine for a moment, then she pulled open the flap. The print she took out was a colour one. She stared down at it. Colour flooded back into her face like a scarlet tide.

'Dear God,' she whispered.

'I'm sorry.' I felt as nervous and inadequate as I ever have, anywhere.

Her unequal eyes slowly came back up to mine. Her voice had gone low and throaty. 'You say this is from an album he kept?'

'Yes.'

Her stare was accusing, now. Her tone changed. 'What do you want?'

'Nothing in the way you are probably thinking. Just some information.'

She put the photo back inside the envelope as though it were infected. Her movements were stiff and shocked; she didn't look up as she spoke. 'What information?'

'I said to you that Ted was helping to dispose of some of the Crockingham Collection. You haven't commented on that.'

'I – I don't know anything about it.' She put the envelope down on a side table, staring at it as though it would bite.

'I'm sorry, but I think you do. Ted was a complex character in many ways. I find that I didn't know him at all well. There's a painting – an oil sketch by Munnings – that he put on his living room wall. I'm sure you've seen it. "Sergeant Murphy and The Drifter". He found it highly symbolic. Sergeant Murphy was the character I knew. Reasonably disciplined, logical, cultured. Once a successful general dealer. Now caught in the depression and the structural changes in the trade. A has-been but still trying. The Drifter was the other symbol for Ted. Always

180

was. I'm sorry to tell you the album has many other entries as well as yours. Taken secretly by a camera behind the dressing table. Ted had a distasteful reverse side. Even his name wasn't really Murphy. It was Pulham.'

'Pulham?' She looked genuinely bewildered. 'His name was Pulham?'

'Apparently. His parents died when he was young. In Dublin. He was brought up in London by distant relatives called Murphy and took their name.'

'I didn't know that.'

'Nor about the album?'

'Of course not!'

'Nor that Angela Hobart was in it?'

'*What?* That whore?'

She almost started from her settee. The nasty death of Angela Hobart wasn't going to affect her sympathy or emotions in any conventional way, obviously. I wondered again at the arrangements and interrelationships at Crockingham Hall; they must have had some extraordinary conversations up there.

'Frank Hobart's wife,' I said, 'had known Ted Murphy for a long time. From before the time when she went to Crockingham. She didn't know about your arrangements with him. I'm talking in both senses now. Your personal arrangement and the arrangement you and Philip had with him to cover your losses at Lloyds.'

She didn't answer. She stared at me, face still white and drawn.

'Sir Andrew loves his collection. He's had it for so long now that he doesn't want to lose it. I bet he doesn't remember everything he bought, not over so long a period. The supplementary things particularly. Profligate collectors can't keep track of everything. James is mostly busy, following Father's footsteps. But Philip had the time, the opportunity and certainly the motive. I wonder; how did he persuade Frank?'

'Angela,' she murmured. 'That bloody bitch. She always needed more money. Frank couldn't help her, not in the luxurious way she wanted, not on his wages.'

'But Sir Andrew? She said he was very generous, in return for, for favours received.'

'Andrew?' She was recovering. Anger had come back to her. 'My father-in-law? He's no hander-out! We went to him first!

Right from the start of this nightmare. He said we were all in the same boat. Couldn't help us any more. Wouldn't help us any more. We were going to lose everything! This' – she gestured at the room – 'the boat, our own cottage, the lot. School fees. Everything. It was ours anyway. Those paintings. No one looked at them. They were going to be ours. We needed them now, not sometime never. We had to have a reserve. So Philip made an arrangement with Frank. He needed to survive too. Angela thought it was Andrew's money, being handed out to her and to Frank for her most obliging – and willing – performance as a concubine. She got mean little presents from Andrew directly, some money as well. But Frank's valuable extras came through us. Through the arrangement with Ted.'

'Oh dear.'

'Then James and Liz said we'd have to sell the Collection. Things were desperate for them, too. They didn't want Andrew to be involved at first. He had to be persuaded later. They made Philip act as go-between. He had to approach Jeremy White.'

'So you had to move quickly then. The supplementary paintings and sketches weren't going to be available much longer.'

'No, they weren't. It was the only cash we could raise.' She looked at me thoughtfully. 'You said that you are the only one who' – she made a hand movement towards the envelope – 'that that's a piece of knowledge only you possess.'

I nodded. 'That's what I said.'

'What are you going to do about it? What else do you know?'

'I know that Frank Hobart put a bomb under my car. He thought that I was going to rumble the fraud you were doing with Ted. On my first visit to Crockingham, I asked him if the catalogue was a complete list and he lied to me. He said yes. I guess Sir Andrew said I was the Fund's investigator and that alarmed him. Frank Hobart had the knowledge to make the bomb from his army days. He was determined to keep the fraud secret. He thought at Snailwell that Angela was telling me about it. That she knew from Ted. That's why he killed her.'

'Wasn't she telling you?'

'Oh, no. She didn't tell me because she didn't know. But Frank was good at following people, wasn't he? Too good, in my case. He must have been told I was coming to Elizabeth Dennison's cottage and he followed me via Cambridge Police Station to the Dun Cow. Very persistent; hours of waiting. I've thought hard about that. Someone must have told him I was due to visit Fen Ditton, and it wasn't James.'

'So you know he killed Elizabeth Dennison?'

'Oh, no. He didn't do it. He wouldn't kill a member of the Carberry family. Never. Philip must have done that. Liz Dennison remembered there was an Orpen in the Collection somewhere. My office painting – at the bank – of Yvonne Aubicq reminded her. James had gone to Crockingham that night; he wasn't at Fen Ditton. When I phoned Elizabeth, someone was with her. Ted Murphy already had the Orpen; he sent me a card about it one day on his way back from Crockingham. He was going to sell it to me. The whole game would be up if Elizabeth told me that there should be an Orpen in the Collection somewhere. So Philip had to have done it.'

'No.' It was a flat denial.

'Yes. He killed Ted, too.' I nodded at the envelope. 'He killed Ted because Ted seduced you while getting you money. That was a domestic matter: straight jealousy. Ted couldn't resist a married woman, neglected, in need of excitement, who spends days and days alone in a flat like this.'

'*No, he couldn't.*'

The voice came from the kitchen doorway. Philip Carberry stood square in the frame as he drew the door back to reveal himself. I gaped at him in genuine astonishment.

'The service entrance,' he said, in answer to my surprise. 'It comes up the kitchen side.'

He was holding an expensive sporting shotgun carefully at waist level, braced in both hands the way an experienced sporting gun user would hold it, casually, when out on a shooting party. The big difference was that it was shut and, almost certainly, loaded.

'Philip.' His wife wasn't as surprised as she might have been. I guessed she must have called him as soon as I'd asked if I could come round. 'How much have you heard?'

'Enough.' He raised the gun to point it at me more menacingly. 'Enough to hear that you, clever fellow, are the only one who possesses this knowledge.'

'You don't dispute it, then?'

He smiled. 'What do you want, a full and frank confession? I'm afraid life's not that easy. But you're doing pretty well.'

'Philip.' His wife's voice was frightened. 'You killed Ted? You?'

He stepped carefully out from the doorway and picked the envelope off the table with his left hand, keeping his trigger finger on the gun. 'What did you expect?' His reply conveyed real hatred as he put his grip back to hold the gun ready for firing. 'Me to sit by and let that seedy Irish crook hump my wife as well as cheat us in business? He was totally dishonest. Said he'd sold for cash, was taking a fair commission, but had already creamed some of the cash off. I couldn't find the rest of it, worse luck, but he'd creamed it all right.'

'And Elizabeth?' I asked.

'My dear sister? My dear independent sister? With her expensive divorce and her boyfriends and superior behaviour? You think I'd let her tell you, you snoop, that there was something missing? I went to ask her to reconsider the sale of the Collection and help persuade James. He wanted too much, anyway; he wouldn't have accepted your offer if she'd held out. No chance; then she starts blabbing to you. Or was going to. I had to stop that.'

'Poor Elizabeth.'

'My father would always have looked after her financially. Not me and Paula. But her. She was his favourite. That's the way it always has been.'

'Oh dear.'

'Oh dear it is. For you.' He held up the envelope. 'Where's that album?'

He raised the shotgun further. I wondered if the thumping of my heart was spoiling reception of the transmission.

'Look outside,' I said. 'There's a van in the street, a white one. It's a police van, recording our conversation from the gadget I've got strapped to my chest, under my shirt. I think you'd better put the shotgun down.'

His face leered. 'Bluff,' he sneered. 'Where's the album? Hoping to make on it, were you?'

There was a faint scuffle behind him in the kitchen and Nobby Roberts came through the door so quickly to put his police pistol on the back of Philip Carberry's neck, that I wondered if he'd touched the floor at all.

Philip Carberry froze at his bidding.

'Service entrance,' Nobby said. 'Thanks for tipping us off

184

about it. We got the message from Tim's gadget perfectly.'

I got up before Philip Carberry had any second thoughts with the shotgun and stood quickly to one side as the twin barrels drooped. Will Cook came in behind Nobby and took the weapon in his capable hands as the standard recitation began.

'Philip Carberry, I am arresting you for the murder of Ted Murphy and Elizabeth Dennison. You do not have to say anything but . . .'

I'd given Nobby the rest of it, just as he wanted.

CHAPTER 26

'I rather thought,' said Sir Richard White, 'that stock write-off fiddles were Andrew Carberry's speciality, not his family's as well. Like father, like son, it seems. Younger son, anyway.'

He grinned at me and winked knowingly across the dinner table, causing Jeremy, at whose board we were feasting, to frown slightly. I responded by picking up my glass and presenting it in a silent toast to the older man before taking an appreciative draught of claret from it.

He toasted me back gallantly.

'I don't think we should talk shop really,' Jeremy said, knowing full well that his wife, Mary, who used to work at the bank, enjoys shop-talk about merchant banking more than anything else. 'Close the hangar doors and all that sort of thing.'

He looked vaguely in Sue's direction as he spoke, but she was happily content with her evening so far. 'Oh, don't mind me,' she said. 'I suppose all's well that ends well. Even if, after all, you have still fetched up with that awful collection of one-horse daubs.'

'Oh, Sue!' Jeremy was quite shocked. 'Don't say that! They're not all of one horse! There's quite a lot of horses in some of them.'

There was a burst of laughter at this, making Jeremy's silver and glass tinkle appreciatively. We were chez White, in the house between Knightsbridge and South Kensington Jeremy has occupied for many years, and the dining room, at the front of the ground floor, looks out on to the thickly-treed square-cum-crescent which is a pleasant feature of the area. On the same floor, the kitchen extends backwards via a handsome conservatory into the small back garden and we have often dined casually there. This, however, was a formal celebration, so the best mahogany dining table had been polished up in our honour.

'The Crockingham Collection,' I said, still smiling, 'will at least come under our own direct sway rather than staying up in the sticks. Further visits to Suffolk will not be required.'

'I should think not,' Sue said, and shivered a little. 'I'll never see beamed old houses the same way again.'

Sir Richard White looked at her sympathetically. 'Alas for Andrew Carberry,' he murmured. 'Rather a lot of tragedy to contend with all at once. His finances are deteriorating by the day. I shouldn't be surprised if he has to sell up and go from there. It would probably be the best thing to do.'

'I'm sure it would. Anyway, I'm not sorry that he waived the request for the Collection to stay put.'

Mary White, for whom I have always had a soft spot, and next to whom I was sitting, turned to me with a questioning expression. 'What has astounded me,' she said, 'is the way in which Andrew Carberry didn't seem to notice what was going out. I mean, surely he must have checked from time to time?'

'Ah,' I said, gratified at the prompting. 'Now is the time to tell you my James Laver story.'

'James Laver story?'

'Yes. He wrote a monograph on Tissot which is a delightful read, even if factually erroneous, but it led me, a while ago, to go on to Laver's volume of memoirs. *Museum Piece*, it's called. There is a glorious patch about collectors in it. Laver says that William Randolph Hearst once saw a photograph of a fine piece of silver in an old catalogue and cabled from California to his representatives in Europe: *Find it. Buy it. Spare no expense.* They spared no expense and after a long interval, cabled back that this particular piece had been in Hearst's own collection for the last ten years.'

I waited until the chuckles had died down and said, 'The point Laver was making was: can one be said to possess a thing one never sees? The supplementary part of the Crockingham Collection was accumulated and put away by Carberry over a long period. Only the things on display really interested him and he's been much too busy a businessman to look at those very much. So it wasn't so difficult to slip things out. Once the Collection was sold, he'd probably never have looked again.'

'And nothing would have emerged.'

'Nothing would have emerged. Although Ted Murphy is an

example of how the best laid plans of mice and men, et cetera, et cetera.'

'How would he have explained the Orpen to you? I mean, if he hadn't been killed and you turned up to buy it?'

I shrugged. 'Most likely as a private acquisition. He could afford to make out an invoice and take a cheque from time to time. And an item on his books called, "Country House Scene", or something like that would then show an enormous profit to delight the taxman with.'

'But it's the Fund's now?'

'It will be. When all the formalities have been completed.'

'And the Munnings oil sketch of "Sergeant Murphy and The Drifter"?'

'That too.'

I found that Sue was looking at me across the table. There was a smile on her face.

'You see,' she said to the others, 'Tim always gets what he's after. And he's been after pictures of Yvonne Aubicq since – since – well, how long is it, Tim?'

I smiled back at her. 'A long time, Sue. Since a very long time ago.'